Dear Reader,

When I was asked to write a book inspired by a fairy tale, I decided to base my story on "The Little Mermaid." I had read about a young woman who is a wild swimming enthusiast and wears a monofin mermaid tail. So I had my real-life mermaid. Arielle is keen to escape the shadow of her father's terrible crimes and when she saves Prince Eirik from drowning, she is drawn to the handsome prince. But she knows she can never be part of Eirik's glamorous world.

I had so much fun creating the Nordic principality of Fjernland that Eirik would soon rule. He is expected to make a suitable marriage and his bride will be his princess consort. But he can't forget the flame-haired siren who has enchanted him. Eirik and Arielle share a passion for marine conservation. As usual, I did far too much research, but I learned about some amazing people involved in initiatives to recycle the huge amounts of plastic waste in the oceans.

I hope you enjoy Arielle and Eirik's story!

Love,

*Chantelle* xxx

**Chantelle Shaw** lives on the Kent coast and thinks up her stories while walking on the beach. She has been married for over thirty years and has six children. Her love affair with reading and writing Harlequin stories began as a teenager, and her first book was published in 2006. She likes strong-willed, slightly unusual characters. Chantelle also loves gardening, walking and wine.

## Books by Chantelle Shaw

### Harlequin Presents

*Wed for the Spaniard's Redemption*
*Proof of Their Forbidden Night*
*Her Wedding Night Negotiation*
*Housekeeper in the Headlines*
*The Italian's Bargain for His Bride*

### ***Innocent Summer Brides***

*The Greek Wedding She Never Had*
*Nine Months to Tame the Tycoon*

Visit the Author Profile page
at Harlequin.com for more titles.

*Chantelle Shaw*

# HER SECRET ROYAL DILEMMA

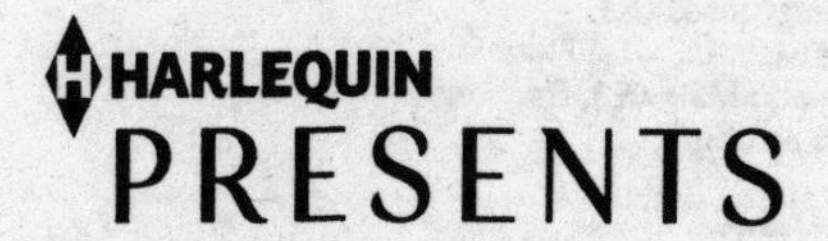

HARLEQUIN® PRESENTS™

Recycling programs for this product may not exist in your area.

ISBN-13: 978-1-335-73853-0

Her Secret Royal Dilemma



For questions and comments about the quality of this book, please contact us at CustomerService@Harlequin.com.

Harlequin Enterprises ULC
22 Adelaide St. West, 41st Floor
Toronto, Ontario M5H 4E3, Canada
www.Harlequin.com

**Printed in U.S.A.**

# HER SECRET ROYAL DILEMMA

# PROLOGUE

THE WAVE WAS MONSTROUS. In the gleam of his head torch, Prince Eirik saw a towering wall of water rise up in front of the yacht. The sea was wild, whipped up by a storm that had arrived earlier than forecast. But this was a rogue wave, spewing white foam as it curled over and began its descent.

Eirik's yacht, *The Mako*, had lost its mast when the storm had first struck an hour or so ago. The VHF antenna had snapped, leaving him without radio signal and unable to put out a Mayday call. Thick clouds prevented the satellite phone from working. He'd had no choice but to abandon the Around the Island of Ireland yacht race, or AII as it was known. The competitors had set sail from the marina at Penash on the south coast of Cornwall. When he had turned back, he'd managed to erect a temporary mast and sail and had been making good headway towards the shore. The craggy Cornish cliffs were close—but not close enough.

Night had brought impenetrable darkness. His head throbbed from where he'd been struck by the mast when it had come crashing down. He pushed his hair out of his eyes, and, in the torchlight, he noticed blood on his fingers from the gash on his brow. He watched the huge wave tumble as if in slow motion towards the deck. The noise filled his ears and reminded him of the roar of the avalanche as it had raced down the mountain.

Had Niels felt afraid? Eirik recalled that fateful day just over a year ago. He had been a few metres ahead of his brother and had managed to ski over to a cluster of pine trees that had given some protection from the avalanche. When he'd looked back at the white wave of snow thundering down the slope, he had known in his heart that Niels would not survive. Eirik's grief was mixed with guilt because he had persuaded his brother to go skiing. They had both loved the slopes when they were younger, but Niels had been the heir to the principality of Fjernland's throne and discouraged by their parents from taking risks.

The world spun, and the starless sky merged with the black sea as the powerful wave caused the yacht to roll one hundred and eighty degrees. After what felt like a lifetime of being churned inside a washing machine *The Mako* righted itself. Coughing and spluttering, Eirik snatched oxygen into his lungs and assessed the new damage. The temporary mast had been destroyed. Fortunately, the compartment where the flares were stored had remained watertight. Distress flares were only meant to be used where there was 'grave and imminent danger to life'.

It was sobering to acknowledge that his situation had become so serious. Moments later he watched a trail of bright red smoke soar into the sky and hoped that someone on land would see the flare and alert the coastguard.

The sea had calmed a little after the freak wave had subsided. A glimmer of moonlight appeared when the clouds parted and showed Eirik that the yacht had drifted closer to the coast. But the bow of the boat was sitting low in the water, and he realised that *The Mako* was sinking. His only chance was to attempt to swim to the shore, but huge breakers crashed against the cliffs, and it was likely that he would be smashed onto the jagged rocks.

He unclipped the safety tether that attached him to the yacht and climbed onto the gunwale. In the moonlight he could just make out the cliffs in the distance. He grimaced. This was a crazy plan, but he was out of options.

It was then that he saw the tail. He knew that dolphins were regularly spotted in the sea around Cornwall. But it hadn't looked like a dolphin's tail. The huge tail broke the surface again, closer to the boat this time, before it disappeared beneath the waves.

Eirik froze and stared at the face that had appeared in the water, a few metres away from the boat. He must be hallucinating. Maybe he was suffering from concussion. He closed his eyes. When he opened them again the creature was still in the sea. A female figure—with a fish's tail? *What the hell?*

She raised her arm and waved to him. Eirik swore.

He did not believe in mystical stories of sea sirens and mermaids, but at that moment he could not think of any other explanation.

'Follow me.' Her voice rose above the noise of the wind. She disappeared beneath the waves and the great tail made a splash.

Water lapped the gunwale. *The Mako* was sinking fast. There was nothing Eirik could do but jump into the sea and swim for his life. The water was bitterly cold, and his body reacted automatically with a gasp reflex that made him choke as his mouth filled with brine. He knew there was a danger that he could develop hypothermia. His chances of survival were slim.

The sea creature, mermaid—whatever she was—surfaced a few metres ahead and beckoned to him. Her skin looked silvery in the moonlight and her face, with its high cheekbones, was as exquisite as a pre-Raphaelite painting. Her long hair streamed behind her as she turned and swam away. Eirik struck out after her. He did not know who or even *what* she was, but she was his only hope.

He had lost his head torch, but the moon was bright now, allowing him to keep sight of the tail when it broke the surface. His chest heaved and his shoulders burned with the effort of swimming. His life jacket helped to keep him afloat, but he could feel the strong current dragging him towards rocks that had appeared, rising out of the sea like terrible, giant's teeth.

Eirik remembered the legends of beautiful sirens

who had led men to their doom. He had been a fool to follow his mystical guide, but he'd never been able to resist a beautiful woman, he thought with grim humour. He was done for. The current was sweeping him closer to the rocks and his will to live was ebbing away as the cold seeped down to his bones.

He felt a hand touch his arm. The mermaid, for want of a better description, was beside him. Her eyes were huge and fathomless in the black night. It occurred to Eirik that perhaps he was already dead and had slipped into some strange underworld.

'Don't give up,' she urged. 'Stay close to me.'

'Who are you?' he shouted after her, but she was already swimming a little way ahead of him. He forced his aching muscles into action and struck out once more.

They seemed to be in a channel of calmer water flowing between the rocks. Waves crashed against the cliffs on either side, but Eirik saw a small cove and a strip of beach in front of him. Dear God! His feet found the seabed and he half crawled, half stumbled out of the waves. His throat felt raw from the salt water he'd swallowed. He sank down onto his knees, coughing and retching, struggling to breathe.

He must have blacked out. When he regained consciousness, his cheek was resting on the wet sand. Someone rolled him over onto his back and supported his head.

'You'll be all right. Please be all right.'

The voice was a lilting melody that Eirik knew

he would never forget. His eyelids felt too heavy for him to open them, and he was cold, so cold.

'Don't go. Don't give up.'

Her voice caught. There was urgency in her song, a tenderness that curled around Eirik's frozen heart. He felt her warm breath on his face, his lips. A hand gently stroked his jaw, and then her mouth covered his. Her lips were soft and moist, easing his lips apart. Her breath filled his mouth. The kiss of an angel, or in this case a mermaid, brought Eirik back from the brink.

He wished he could stay in her embrace for ever. He opened his eyes and stared into her fathomless dark gaze. Instantly she snatched her mouth from his and lowered his head onto the sand. By the time he'd propped himself up onto one elbow, his saviour had returned to the sea and was sitting on a partly submerged rock. It was impossible to make out the colour of her wet hair that rippled over her shoulders. Her tail—yes, it was definitely a *tail*—sparkled silver in the moonlight.

'Who are you?' he rasped.

'You are safe now. Help will come,' she told him in her sweet voice before she dived into the waves.

'Wait.' Eirik stared after her, but she had gone. Had he imagined her? His logical brain argued that he must have done. But without her guidance he would not have found his way to the cove.

He fell back against the sand and drifted in and out of consciousness. Some time later, it could have been minutes or hours, he heard the womp, womp of a helicopter's rotor blades in the sky above him. Shielding his eyes against the glare of the searchlight, he watched a medic being winched down to the beach.

'Your Royal Highness, your aides will be relieved that you are safe,' the medic told him. 'There was great concern after radio contact with you was lost. It was an incredible chance that you found your way to Pixie Cove. Only a few people who live in these parts know that the sea around the cove is more sheltered than the rest of the coastline.'

Pixie Cove! The name was apt, Eirik thought. He pushed his fingers through his hair that was matted with salt and blood. 'It wasn't luck,' he muttered. 'I know it sounds crazy, but I was guided by a… mermaid.'

It sounded ridiculous and he expected the medic to laugh or at least reassure him that he was suffering from concussion. But the man was surprisingly unsurprised.

'Ah, Cornwall's very own mermaid. I've not seen her myself, but I have heard of Arielle.'

# CHAPTER ONE

'EVEN YOU MUST admit that Prince Eirik is lush.'

The jeering voice startled Arielle, and she flushed when she realised that she had been caught staring at the handsome hunk across the lawn who was attracting admiring looks from every female present. She glanced at the woman who had come to stand beside her.

'Even me?' She was automatically defensive. Tamara Bray was a prize bitch and had been the leader of the gang of bullies who'd made Arielle's school days hell.

'You have never shown an interest in any of the men who live around here, but none of them would want to get involved with the daughter of a convicted criminal. Do you really think a nobody like you would stand a chance with the Prince?' Tamara had a good reason to hate Arielle's father for what he had done. In his absence she had directed her spite at Arielle and the name-calling when they had been teenagers had turned into something much nastier. 'Mind you, none of the local guys look like *him*.'

Arielle followed Tamara's gaze back across the garden to where His Royal Highness, Prince Eirik of Fjernland was chatting to the commodore of the yacht club. Undoubtedly the Prince was *lush*—a West Country expression to describe a good-looking person. The Prince was a golden god with his tousled, dark blond hair and skin tanned to the colour of honey. The surgical dressing on his forehead did not detract from his handsome features.

In the past, photos of the dissolute, playboy prince had regularly appeared in the tabloids, although since his brother's death Prince Eirik had dropped out of the media spotlight. Arielle had developed a bit of a crush on him, to be honest. She'd cut out his picture from the pages of a celebrity magazine and stuck it on the fridge. Every time she opened the door, she noticed his mesmerising eyes, which were the same shade of bright blue as the Cornish sky on this crisp, spring day.

The breeze blowing off the sea tugged at Arielle's hair, which she'd piled on top of her head in an attempt to look respectable. An errant auburn curl brushed against her cheek, and she lifted her hand to tuck it behind her ear. Her eyes were still fixed on Prince Eirik.

He looked a lot better than he had done three nights ago when she'd guided him through the rough sea to Pixie Cove. She had been concerned for him when she'd left him on the beach and gone to get help. When she'd seen a news report that the Prince had been airlifted to hospital in Penzance after he'd nearly drowned at sea, she had felt relieved that he was safe.

Prince Eirik's tall and imposing presence made him stand out from the other guests at the yacht club who flocked around him. His impressive, muscular physique and the thick blond stubble on his jaw were an indication of his Viking ancestry.

'Where is Fjernland anyway?' Tamara muttered. 'I used to bunk off geography lessons.'

'It's an island in the North Sea between the Danish peninsular of Jutland and the coast of southern Norway,' Arielle explained. 'Historically, Denmark made repeated attempts to control Fjernland, but Fjernlandic men were reputed to have been the most fearsome and pitiless of all the Norse warriors and the island became an independent principality some time in the tenth century. The current monarch is His Serene Highness, Prince Otto III, who rules with his wife and consort Princess Hulda. Prince Eirik is their only surviving son and heir after the death of his older brother, Prince Niels.'

'You always were a swot. But even though you've got a fancy degree, your dad is a murderer, and a lot of people around here think you should be in prison too,' Tamara said viciously.

'I knew nothing about my father's activities or what happened to your cousin.'

'Yeah, right.'

Tension twisted in a knot in the pit of Arielle's stomach at Tamara's mention of her father. She felt that she could never escape from her past. She looked towards the marina, where the yachts that had taken part in the famous Around the Island of Ireland sailing race were moored. All the boats had completed the race within forty-eight hours, with one notable exception. Prince Eirik's accident had made the international news headlines, but thankfully there had been no mention of Arielle's involvement. The last thing she wanted was to attract the attention of the press.

The clink of rigging carried on the breeze, and the boats bobbed on the swell. The salty tang of the sea made Arielle impatient to go swimming. She swam and free-dived wearing a monofin most days. The sea was her second home, and she was a strong swimmer, but the confidence she felt in the ocean was non-existent in every other area of her life.

The villagers thought she was as reclusive as her father when he'd lived at the cliff-top cottage that had been Arielle's home all her life. It was hardly surprising she kept herself to herself, she thought bitterly. Gerran Rowse's reputation as a troublemaker had caused people to shun Arielle, and her mother when she had been alive.

Arielle did not fit in anywhere, certainly not at the exclusive yacht club. The members were mostly wealthy, retired professionals who had swapped city life for a coastal idyll and bemoaned the lack of a well-known coffee-shop chain. None of the local fishermen who took their trawlers out to sea to make a precarious living belonged to the yacht club. But Arielle was not part of Penash's tight-knit fishing community either. The men who had visited her father in the middle of the night had moored their boats further along the coast.

She had been surprised when the commodore of the yacht club had turned up at her studio the previous day.

'The Prince of Fjernland has left hospital following his ordeal at sea and he will present the prize to the winner of the AII race,' Charles Daventry had told her. 'I have been informed by Prince Eirik's private secretary that His Royal Highness would like to meet you.'

Arielle's heart had given a jolt. 'Why does he want to meet *me*?' She'd wondered if the Prince had found out that she had helped him, although she had not told anyone. But then she'd had the sickening thought that he might be curious about her father's notoriety. The press had hounded her after Gerran Rowse's conviction and it was one reason why Arielle had changed her surname.

'Prince Eirik is passionate about marine conservation,' Charles had explained. 'He supports the International Clean Sea campaign, and he heard about your project to recycle plastic waste collected from the ocean and turn it into decorative items.'

Charles had picked up a coaster that Arielle had made from recycled plastic granules and studied it with a perplexed expression. 'The committee have decided to ask you to bring some of your products to the yacht club. If the Prince has time after the prize-giving ceremony he might want to take a look at them.'

Publicity for marine conservation was always a good thing, Arielle had reminded herself when she'd arrived at the clubhouse earlier. The guests had still been having lunch and a snooty steward had directed her outside to a table set up on the lawn where she could display her work. Some other local businesses had also been invited and Tamara was there to represent her father's company.

Tamara gave Arielle a dirty look before she walked over to a table bearing crates of beer labelled Bray's Brewery. 'Why don't you do everyone a favour and clear off? I don't know why you are even here.'

'Apparently the Prince is interested in my plastics recycling initiative.'

'The Prince is not going to be interested in anything you have to say. If his security team have discovered that your father is a convicted criminal, they probably won't let you near him.'

Arielle was stung by Tamara's comments. She had endured years of being made to feel worthless by her father. Anger and resentment bubbled up inside her. She had done nothing wrong but nevertheless she'd been ostracised by the villagers. Her conscience pricked that she should have tried harder to discover the truth about her father's shady business dealings. The smallholding where he'd kept mainly sheep had not been profitable, but once Arielle had found a holdall stuffed full of bank notes hidden behind some hay bales. When strangers had come to the cottage, she had locked herself in her bedroom as her father had told her to do.

Automatically she lifted her hand and traced her finger over the faint ridge of a scar on her cheek. Her father was serving a life sentence in prison, and she no longer had to fear him, but she was haunted by his scandalous crimes.

Tamara was right. Prince Eirik would not be interested in anything she had to say, Arielle thought bleakly. The Prince's jet-setting lifestyle was one long round of lavish parties, from what she'd read about him. He was feted and adored wherever he went, and his legendary charm attracted women like bees to honey. But not this woman, she told herself.

'Prince Eirik is walking this way,' Tamara said excitedly. 'I can't believe I'm going to meet a real prince.'

Arielle watched the Prince stride across the lawn. He ignored Tamara and made a beeline for her. His tall figure blocked out the sun and she had to tilt her head to look at his face. Her eyes crashed with his glittering gaze, and she saw a flash of recognition in their blue depths.

'*You!* You're the mermaid.' He sounded stunned. He stepped closer to her, his eyes searching her face intently. 'Who *are* you?' Before Arielle could answer, Prince Eirik glanced over his shoulder and cursed when he saw his retinue of aides hurrying across the lawn after him. 'I told myself that I had imagined you. But you are a real woman.' He ran his eyes over her, and something in the way he looked at her sent a rush of heat through Arielle's veins.

He was even more gorgeous than she remembered from three nights ago. She had cradled his head in her lap and there had been a vulnerability to him then that had tugged on her heart. Now he appeared to be fully recovered from his ordeal in the sea and his male potency stirred an age-old feminine response low in her pelvis.

She estimated that he was three or four inches over six feet tall. The pale blue shirt stretched across his torso was unbuttoned at the throat to show a sprinkling of blond chest hairs. Arielle lowered her gaze and made a quick inventory of his narrow hips and long legs encased in slim-fit navy blue trousers. His whipcord body exuded strength and power. She lifted her eyes to his face once more and the gleam in his eyes made her heart miss a beat.

'You saved my life.' He swore softly when he saw the commodore bearing down on them. 'I want to talk to you,' he told Arielle in a low tone. 'But not here. Is there somewhere where we can be alone?'

'I don't think so,' she murmured, thinking that the press photographers who were at the yacht club would be wildly curious if Prince Eirik took her off for a private conversation.

He hid his frustration with obvious effort when Charles Daventry halted next to Arielle's table and made introductions.

'Your Highness, this is Arielle Tremain, who is involved with the Clean Sea organisation.'

Arielle held out her hand to the Prince and murmured, 'I'm pleased to meet you, Your Royal Highness.'

Out of the corner of her eye she saw Charles frown and belatedly remembered that she had been instructed to curtsey to the Prince. But before she could attempt the manoeuvre, Prince Eirik curled his strong fingers around her hand and a sensation like an electrical current shot up her arm.

'Arielle…' His husky accent was spine-tinglingly sexy. 'You have a beautiful name. It suits you.'

His smile stole her breath, and the tingling sensation spread to her breasts. Her nipples tightened and she was conscious of her lacy bra scraping against the sensitive tips. For once she was wearing a dress instead of jeans and a shapeless sweatshirt, which were her usual choice of clothes. She spent most days alone in her workshop, but for her visit to the yacht club she had dug out the only dress she owned. It was a bit tighter over her bust than she'd remembered and a hasty downwards glance revealed the faint outline of her nipples beneath the clingy material.

Arielle wished she could cross her arms over her chest to hide her body's unbidden response to Prince Eirik, but her hand was still trapped in his firm grasp. Sensual heat suffused her as he roamed his eyes over her figure. She was surprised by her reaction to him. It was two years since she'd finished with Jack and sworn off men.

The Prince was an exceptional man, and she could be forgiven for being dazzled by his stunning good looks and charisma, Arielle consoled herself. He was a notorious womaniser and flirting was second nature to him.

Their eyes met and she felt a jolt of awareness. It was as though time were suspended, and the crowd of people in the garden disappeared, leaving her and the Prince beneath the wide blue sky. He was a work of art with those sculpted cheekbones and a mouth that was blatantly inviting.

She knew about his mouth; the sensual curve of his lips and the way they had fitted against hers. He had been semi-conscious, and she had acted to revive him. It was unlikely he remembered, she reassured herself, but the wicked gleam in his laser blue eyes caused her heart to crash against her ribs.

A discreet cough from the commodore broke the spell that Prince Eirik had cast on Arielle and with a faint gasp she snatched her hand out of his. To her relief he released her from his mesmerising stare, and she quickly moved away to stand behind her table. The Prince looked down at the items on display.

'You made all these things from recycled plastic? I'm impressed,' he murmured when she nodded.

'I mostly make small items such as key fobs, coasters and jewellery.' She picked up a pair of cufflinks and offered them to him. 'It's hard to believe that these were once crisp packets or other unrecyclable plastic. The plastic waste is processed through a granulator into a fine aggregate, which is mixed with a plant-based resin binder before it can be cast into the products you see here.'

The Prince lifted a necklace from a display stand. It was one of Arielle's favourite pieces, and had an intricate chain interspersed with tiny teardrop resin pendants. 'Who is responsible for the silverwork on the jewellery?'

'Me.' Her face grew warm beneath his intent gaze. 'I taught myself silversmithing through trial and error. Mostly error at first,' she admitted ruefully.

Prince Eirik leaned across the table and stretched out his hand to touch the green glass earring dangling from Arielle's earlobe. 'Did you make the pair of earrings you are wearing? They match the colour of your eyes.'

His face was so close to hers that she felt his warm breath on her cheek. The spicy scent of his cologne teased her senses. 'Yes.' Her voice emerged as a smoky whisper. She cleared her throat. 'As well as plastic I collect sea glass from the beach and use it to make jewellery, which I sell online.'

'You are full of surprises, Arielle,' he drawled.

She tensed, wondering if he had heard the local gossip about her father's crimes. 'What do you mean?'

His eyes narrowed. 'I understand that you organise the collection of plastic and other rubbish from local beaches.'

'Oh.' She released her breath slowly. 'Yes, I take part in regular beach cleans and encourage other people to help out.'

'I have campaigned for a similar scheme to be adopted in Fjernland.' Prince Eirik gave Arielle a thoughtful look and she was sure she had not imagined the sizzle of attraction between them.

While they had been talking, Tamara had pushed her way to the front of the crowd of people standing near the Prince. She dipped into a sweeping curtsey while the commodore introduced her.

'Your Royal Highness, it is an honour to meet you. I am a close friend of Arielle and I'm deeply committed to saving our oceans from plastic waste,' Tamara told him earnestly. She managed to simultaneously smile at the Prince and shoot a warning look at Arielle.

Seriously! Arielle almost laughed out loud at Tamara's blatant lies. She had never helped out at a beach-clean event. More people had crowded around Prince Eirik and Tamara was fluttering her eyelashes at him like a demented moth.

The Prince looked back at Arielle. 'I would have liked the opportunity to discuss your work with the Clean Sea project in more detail,' he murmured before he was ushered away by the commodore to greet other local business leaders.

Arielle packed up her products and drove home in a strange mood. Meeting Prince Eirik had left her feeling restless and dissatisfied with her life. Tamara's words echoed inside her head. *'Do you really think a nobody like you would stand a chance with the Prince?'*

Well, no, Arielle hadn't expected that he would notice her, and she certainly wouldn't admit to having a secret fantasy where the handsome prince saved her from her dead-end life. Prince Eirik had seemed genuinely interested in her plastics recycling initiative. He had treated her as an equal and listened to what she had to say, which was more than her father or the villagers of Penash had ever done. Living here, she would always be tainted by her father's crimes.

Something inside her had changed and she vowed not to waste any more of her life waiting for a prince to rescue her. The cliff-top cottage held happy memories of her mother. But there had been sadness and despair within the cottage's thick walls and the spilled blood of an innocent man. For as long as she could remember, Arielle had been under the influence of her father. He had been in prison for the last three years, but she had been trapped in a prison of her own making.

Meeting the Prince had given her a glimpse of a world where she did not feel judged, and she was determined to make a new life for herself far away from Penash.

## CHAPTER TWO

THAT NEW DRESS FEELING! Arielle's doubts multiplied as she fiddled with the narrow shoulder straps on the black silk jersey dress. She frowned at her reflection in the mirror, dismayed by the amount of her flesh on display. The skirt was too short, and the neckline was more low-cut than she remembered from when she'd tried the dress on in the boutique.

She was tempted to change into her faithful navy blue dress that she'd bought four years ago for her graduation ceremony from university. Since then, it had lived at the back of her wardrobe. She'd worn it to a couple of job interviews and to the event at the yacht club earlier in the day when she had met Prince Eirik, hence the need for a new outfit.

An invitation to have dinner with the Prince had sent her hurrying off to Truro in search of something suitable to wear. Her aim had been to look sophisticated, but the dress screamed available and possibly even desperate.

She picked up the gold-edged card from the mantelpiece and her eyes followed the bold handwriting inviting her to dine with the Prince at his hotel. A handwritten note was unusual these days, when most people communicated electronically by email or text. It was signed informally Eirik, and the sight of his name set butterflies loose in Arielle's stomach.

Soon after she had returned home from the yacht club, a limousine with dark-tinted windows had stopped in front of her cottage, and a man who she did not recognise had got out and knocked on the front door. Arielle had hidden behind the curtains. Memories of strangers who had arrived in cars with blacked-out windows to do secret business with her father made her feel tense. She had learned at his trial that Gerran Rowse had been a major drugs dealer and the mastermind behind an operation to smuggle huge quantities of heroin and cocaine into Cornwall on fishing boats.

But her father would spend the rest of his life behind bars, and Arielle had resolved not to live in fear any more. She'd opened the front door, prepared to tell the stranger to clear off. The smartly dressed man, greying at his temples, had introduced himself as Gustav Koch, Private Secretary to His Royal Highness, Prince Eirik.

'It is the Prince's wish that I convey your answer to him,' he had told Arielle after she'd read the invitation. 'He very much hopes that you will accept.' Gustav's inscrutable expression had not altered, but Arielle had noticed him glance at her scruffy jeans and sweatshirt that she had changed into because she'd planned to spend the afternoon working in her studio. Perhaps the royal assistant did not think she was good enough to meet the Prince.

Her chin had come up. 'Dinner will be lovely,' she had heard herself say before she'd had time to think of an excuse to decline.

'Good. A car will collect you at seven thirty.'

It was nearly that now, and there was not enough time to change her dress or make another attempt to gather her hair up in a chignon. Her curls were always especially rebellious after she'd just washed her hair. Car headlights shone through the window. Cinderella's coach had arrived. Arielle's heart gave a lurch of nervous excitement. She wrapped the green silk shawl that had belonged to her mother around her shoulders and picked up her evening purse.

She had bought her first pair of stiletto shoes to wear with the new dress and wished she had practised walking in high heels when she stepped outside and made her way gingerly across the cobblestones to the waiting car. The chauffeur held open the door and she slid onto the back seat. The interior of the car smelled of plush leather and the faint but distinctive scent of the Prince's aftershave.

Her stomach muscles involuntarily clenched at the prospect of seeing Prince Eirik again. But she reminded herself that he had said he wanted to discuss the Clean Sea campaign to rid the ocean of plastic waste. It was likely that he had invited other guests who were involved with the campaign to the dinner party.

The hotel a few miles along the coast from Penash

was the most exclusive place to stay in Cornwall. The car turned onto the driveway but instead of stopping in front of the grand entrance, the chauffeur drove around to the back of the hotel. 'I was instructed to bring you this way,' he explained as he ushered Arielle through a door next to the kitchens. They walked along a corridor where there was a strong smell of cooking. 'Wait here,' the driver told her. 'I will tell Gustav that you have arrived.'

Had the Prince's private secretary been concerned that she might wear her old jeans, and that was the reason she been brought into the hotel unseen? Arielle wondered. The chauffeur had strolled further up the corridor and was holding his phone to his ear. The door to the kitchen swung open and a young man dressed in chef whites walked out.

'Well, if it isn't Arielle Rowse,' he said in an unpleasant voice when he saw her.

'Tremain,' she corrected him quickly. But Tamara Bray's brother, Danny, shook his head. 'You might have changed your name, but it doesn't change who your father is. Gerran killed my cousin Josh, and you did nothing to stop him.'

'I didn't know…' Arielle broke off. There was no point trying to defend herself. A few people in Penash thought she had been involved in her father's drug-dealing operation and Danny and his family believed she had known that Gerran had shot and killed a local police constable.

'What are you doing at the hotel all dolled up?' Danny ran his eyes over her dress.

'I'm having dinner here,' Arielle said abruptly. She wasn't going to reveal that she would be meeting Prince Eirik.

'I'm surprised you can afford the Belvedere's prices. But maybe you are up to your dad's old tricks. A fancy car was seen driving up to your place.' Danny shrugged. 'The police never found the last consignment of drugs that Gerran smuggled into Cornwall before he was arrested. I reckon you know where he hid the stuff and you've been waiting for interest in the story to fade before you could carry on his drug-dealing business. All that collecting plastic from the beach and recycling it to make table mats is just a front to hide what you're really doing.'

'None of that is true.' Arielle panicked when she spotted Gustav walking across the hotel foyer. She feared Danny might make more vile accusations and be overheard. 'Get lost, Danny,' she muttered before she hurried away from him.

'Miss Tremain, please come with me.' Gustav directed her into the service lift that was used by the staff. 'I apologise for the secrecy, but there are journalists outside the front of the hotel. Prince Eirik's yachting accident has unfortunately made the headlines around the world.' The lift stopped at the top floor, and they stepped directly into the penthouse suite. 'I'll let the Prince know you are here,' Gustav murmured before he disappeared through a door.

Arielle looked around the elegantly furnished sitting room. She had never been in such luxurious surroundings and felt out of her depth. The conversation with Danny had been a painful reminder of her father's crimes and she felt tainted by her association with him. She was tempted to leave before the Prince's other guests arrived. No one would notice if she slipped out of the hotel through the back door. But a stubborn voice inside her insisted that she had nothing to be ashamed of.

Her heels sank into the deep-pile carpet as she walked over to the huge window that gave wonderful views of the bay. In the moonlight, the sea was as calm as a pond.

'It looks benign, doesn't it?' The gravelly voice from behind Arielle sent a quiver along her spine. 'It's hard to believe that the sea was so wild the other night and my yacht was destroyed by powerful waves.'

'I love its unpredictability. Only a fool believes the oceans can be controlled,' Arielle said softly. Her heart was banging against her ribs, and she could not bring herself to turn around immediately. But then she remembered that he was a *prince*. She spun away from the window and almost overbalanced in her high heels before making a clumsy attempt at a curtsey. 'Your Highness.'

'Please, no formality.' Prince Eirik crossed the room in long strides and stopped in front of her. 'I recognised your voice. When you appeared among the waves the other night, I thought I was hallucinating.' His eyes were the brightest blue imaginable, and he was completely gorgeous. Arielle was unprepared for his devastating impact on her when he smiled.

'It sounds crazy,' he said ruefully, 'but when I saw that you had a tail and silvery skin, I half believed you were an actual mermaid.'

She laughed. 'I was wearing a silver wetsuit, and I swim with a monofin. I'd love to be a real mermaid, but I have legs.'

'I noticed,' the Prince said in a low tone that sent a spike of heat through Arielle. The brilliant gleam in his eyes made her catch her breath as he roamed his gaze over her and lingered on the swell of her breasts, before moving lower to make a leisurely appraisal of her legs.

She prayed there wasn't a snag in her ultra-fine stockings that she'd picked up by mistake when she'd meant to buy a pair of tights. She was conscious of the bare skin at the tops of her thighs above the wide bands of lace that held the stockings up. Shockingly she felt a slick dampness between her legs as she imagined the Prince lifting her dress and sliding his hand over her naked thighs.

Something raw and feral blazed in his eyes. Arielle was mortified that he might have read her mind. 'Forgive me, I am forgetting my manners,' he said abruptly. He shoved his hand through his dark blond hair and walked over to a table where there was a bottle in an ice bucket and two glasses. Arielle's gaze followed him. He looked incredibly attractive in tailored black trousers and a cream shirt made of a filmy material, through which she could faintly see his golden skin and the darker shadow of his chest hairs.

'Would you like some champagne?'

'That will be lovely.' At least she supposed it would. She'd never tried champagne before. The Prince popped the cork on the bottle and filled a long flute with pale golden bubbles.

'Unfortunately, I can't join you,' he said as he handed Arielle her drink before he poured himself a glass of sparkling water. 'My doctor is concerned that the wound on my head could become infected and has insisted I take a course of antibiotics.'

He was no longer wearing the surgical dressing. Her eyes flew to the red weal on his brow where the cut had obviously been stitched. 'I suppose you can't take risks with your health now you are the heir to Fjernland's throne.'

She could have kicked herself for being so blunt when his expression became shuttered. It was only just over a year since the tragic death of his older brother, she remembered.

'Quite so,' the Prince said drily. 'Only a few of my closest aides knew that I was competing in the AII race. The news that my yacht had sunk in treacherous sea conditions was not well received by Their Serene Highnesses.' He noticed Arielle's look of surprise that he had referred to his parents by their formal titles and raised a quizzical eyebrow. 'The Sovereign Prince and Princess are monarchs first and foremost. When I was growing up, parenting me was low down on their list of priorities.' There was faint bitterness in his voice.

Arielle took a sip of champagne and blinked as

the tiny bubbles exploded in her mouth. She'd read somewhere that you couldn't get drunk on champagne, but she did not intend to put the theory to the test. She hoped the Prince hadn't opened the bottle just for her. 'I expect your other guests will drink the champagne.'

'Other guests?' He shook his head. 'There are no other guests. I wanted to meet you privately and we will have dinner here in my suite. But if you prefer, we can go down to the public dining room.'

And risk being spotted by someone from the press or by Danny Bray? She quickly shook her head. 'Here is fine.' She hesitated. 'Should I address you as Your Highness or Prince Eirik?'

He smiled, showing a flash of brilliant white teeth in his tanned face, and her heart collided with her ribs again. 'Eirik will do nicely—Arielle.' His husky accent turned her name into a song. Her skin burned where he placed his hand at the base of her spine and escorted her into the private dining room. 'Allow me,' he murmured as he lifted her silk shawl from her shoulders.

His fingers lightly brushed against her skin, and she felt as though he had branded her. Get a grip, Arielle told herself sternly. Maybe the champagne would help her to relax, she thought, and took a gulp of her drink.

Eirik took his place opposite Arielle at the table. She had tensed when he'd pulled out her chair and waited for her to sit down and he wondered why she was wary of him. It was not a reaction he usually evoked in women. He found her intriguing and the sexual chemistry between them was almost tangible.

She took several sips of her champagne, reinforcing his idea that she was nervous. It was difficult to believe after she had demonstrated incredible bravery when she'd swum out to his sinking yacht and guided him to safety. But the fact that he was not only royal but the heir to the throne tended to create a distance between him and other people.

When he had been the spare heir, he'd largely been left to his own devices and had enjoyed more freedom than his brother. Sometimes he'd felt guilty that Niels had borne the burden of being Fjernland's future monarch with all the expectation and weight of history on his shoulders. It was not a role that Eirik had ever wanted, and he'd been able to avoid much of the pomp and ceremony of royal life and focus on establishing his yacht-manufacturing company.

All that had changed on the mountain. From now on his life would be dictated by protocol and ceremony and above all duty to the crown. The very existence of Fjernland as a principality rested on Eirik's shoulders. According to the laws of succession, if the monarch died without an heir, Fjernland would lose its independent status that it had won in bloody battles many centuries ago and would once again be ruled by Denmark.

Eirik accepted that he must marry. It was not a prospect that filled him with pleasure, but that hardly mattered. He had been responsible for his brother's death—certainly that was his mother's opinion. He was under pressure to choose a suitably aristocratic wife and produce an heir as soon as possible, in preparation for when he became ruler of Fjernland.

Tonight was his last opportunity to have dinner with a beautiful young woman who was not in any way a contender to be his wife. Thinking of the future made him want to numb his mind with champagne, or even better spend a few hours in the arms of the sexy redhead whose sea green eyes hinted at a sensuality he was eager to explore. Was one last night of pleasure with no strings attached too much to wish for?

He shifted position in his seat as his arousal pressed uncomfortably against the zip on his trousers. He had been instantly turned on when he'd walked into the sitting room and studied Arielle's toned figure in a dress that was no more than a wisp of black silk, which showed off her full breasts and long, slender legs. As for that hair! He longed to bury his fingers in her riotous red curls that tumbled to halfway down her back.

Silently cursing his libido that had inconveniently sprung into life after more than a year's absence, Eirik was relieved when there was a knock on the door and Gustav entered the suite, followed by a team of waiters who served dinner. One of them topped up Arielle's glass with champagne.

Eirik caught his private secretary's eye. 'See to it that we are not disturbed for the rest of the evening, will you?'

'Of course, sir,' Gustav replied smoothly.

Eirik heard faint disapproval in his chief aide's voice. He had lived like a monk for over a year, and he was aware that if the media learned of an indiscretion with a woman they might resurrect his reputation—not wholly undeserved of a playboy prince. Eirik trusted Gustav, whom he regarded as a friend as much as an employee. But his brush with death had left him feeling reckless.

After the staff had left, Arielle drank more champagne. There was a soft flush on her cheeks and Eirik noticed that her hand trembled when she put down her glass. Wanting to help her feel at ease, he kept the conversation light and told her a little about his country.

'The North Sea around Fjernland's coast is never very warm to swim in, even in summer. But the country is a volcanic island and has numerous hot springs. If you ever get the chance to visit, I think you would enjoy the lakes, which are heated by geothermal activity. There would be no need for you to wear a wetsuit for swimming.'

His gaze was drawn to the pale curves of her breasts above the low-cut bodice of her dress, and he imagined her wearing a skimpy bikini. The atmosphere in the room crackled with electricity. His body tightened as he watched a pink stain spread across Arielle's face and down her throat and décolletage. Eirik could not remember the last time he'd seen a woman blush. Arielle's unworldly air fired his curiosity, and her sexy curves fanned the flames of his desire.

'The sight of a mermaid swimming in the clear water of the Crystal Lagoon, which is Fjernland's most famous beauty spot, would definitely be a newsworthy story,' he murmured. 'In fact, I am surprised that you are not a celebrity here in Cornwall.'

An odd expression flickered on her face. 'Ah, but mermaids are shy and elusive creatures who prefer to stay out of the limelight.'

She put down her knife and fork even though she had barely touched her dinner. Eirik hadn't eaten much either, although the lobster gratin was exceptionally good. His appetite had disappeared, and he felt hunger of a different kind.

'How did you know my yacht was in trouble? It was astonishing that you were able to find me in the dark when the sea was so rough.'

'I didn't realise it was you who had let off a flare, I just knew that someone was in trouble. Earlier in the day the weather had been quite calm when I swam around the headland. I'd left my clothes and phone hidden in a cave on the main beach. Pixie Cove is only accessible from the sea as the cliffs are too steep to climb and I was trapped there for a few hours until the storm passed.'

Arielle paused and tucked an auburn curl behind her ear. 'When I saw the flare, I had no way of alerting the coastguard. I hoped that someone else had spotted it, but I didn't see the helicopter, so I decided to swim back to where I'd left my phone. But

I saw a tiny light further out to sea and swam out to investigate.'

'I knew my only chance of survival was to try to swim to the shore, but I would never have made it without you to guide me,' Eirik said gruffly. 'The waves were huge, and I would have been thrown against the rocks. When I saw a woman with a fish-tail swimming in the sea, I told myself I was imagining things.'

'As soon as you had made it to the cove and I knew you were safe, I swam back to where I'd left my phone and called the emergency services.'

'Why do you use a monofin?'

'It helps me to swim greater distances and enables me to free-dive deeper. I don't use scuba gear. The dolphin-kick motion when I am wearing a monofin is quite different from conventional swimming and allows me to conserve energy and swim more powerfully.'

'Do you compete at swimming events?'

'I don't care about winning races. I learned to swim before I could walk. My mother passed her love of the sea on to me. She died when I was a child, but I feel close to her when I am in the ocean.'

Eirik had heard a tremor in her voice. 'That must have been tough. Who took care of you after your mother passed away?'

Arielle drained the last of the champagne from her glass. 'I lived with my father, but he is not around now.'

Eirik sensed that she did not want to talk about

her family. She was young to have lost both her parents, and he knew that grief could be consuming.

'Would you like dessert?' He indicated the sweet trolley. The gateau oozing with cream looked sickly, and he wasn't surprised when she declined. 'Let's take our coffee outside,' he suggested. 'It's fairly warm this evening, and there is underfloor heating on the terrace.'

He carried the tray with a cafetière and cups out onto the balcony, set it down on the table and poured the coffee.

Arielle followed and looked at him uncertainly. 'Shouldn't I serve you, seeing as you are a prince?'

'I'm capable of pouring coffee,' he said drily. 'I was fortunate to escape the stifling court etiquette and go to university in America. It gave me the chance to live a normal life and learn to fend for myself. As a matter of fact, I'm not a bad cook.'

Rattan furniture was arranged around a low table on the balcony. Eirik sat down on the sofa and was amused when Arielle claimed the armchair furthest away from him. Most women would have taken the opportunity to sit beside him and perhaps lean in close or play with their hair. He was used to the flirtatious games that women played. He'd been aware of the glances Arielle had sent him across the dinner table when she'd thought he hadn't noticed. If her cool reserve was intended to fuel his interest it was working.

He leaned back against the cushions and stretched his long legs out in front of him. It was a clear night, and the sky was studded with glittering stars that multiplied when you tried to count them. The sound of the waves rippling onto the shore should have been soothing, but Eirik had never felt less soothed in his life. He forced his thoughts away from the carnal impact of Arielle's mouth that had driven him to distraction throughout dinner.

'I suppose your love of the sea led to your support of the Clean Sea campaign to rid the oceans of plastic waste.'

She nodded. 'I always knew I wanted a career that involved the sea and I have a degree in ocean science and marine conservation. I was employed for a year on a local project that involved underwater clean-ups, mainly plastic litter, and discarded fishing equipment. But the money for the project ran out.'

She sighed. 'Marine conservation is underfunded and there is a lack of job opportunities in Cornwall. I started making products from unrecyclable plastic waste and I belong to a collective, trading under the name Plastic-Free Sea. Fifty per cent of our profits go towards marine conservation projects. Obviously, there are production costs to consider.' She gave a rueful smile. 'I'll never be rich. The work of PFS and similar organisations barely touches the mountain of plastic waste in the oceans, but it's better than nothing.'

Eirik found himself captivated by Arielle's enthusiasm for her work. Would she exhibit the same fire and passion in bed? he wondered. He swore silently, irritated by his apparently one-track mind.

'Have you thought about looking for a job in marine conservation further afield? Fjernland is an island, and a healthy ocean environment is important to all Fjernlanders. But, unfortunately, the focus on marine issues has, until recently, lagged behind other countries.'

One hundred years ago, the principality had changed from an absolute monarchy and adopted a constitution, but the Sovereign Prince was also Head of State and still retained much of the governing power, although there were some judicial and legislative branches of government. Eirik had often felt frustrated by his father's lack of foresight in a rapidly changing world. Niels had understood the ecological problems that Fjernland faced and had supported Eirik's efforts to promote the principality as a leader in conservation.

'Five years ago, my brother and I established the Fjernland Marine Research Institute. The organisation employs people with a range of knowledge and expertise. I am sure there must be opportunities around the world for someone with your qualifications and enthusiasm.'

'You're right,' Arielle said in a low voice. 'I have seen advertisements for marine conservation jobs abroad. I even began the application process for a couple of positions, but I always came up with an excuse to withdraw my CV.'

She stood up and walked over to the balcony rail, standing with her back towards Eirik as she stared at the moonlit sea. He admired her derrière where her dress clung to her shapely curves. She was a mystery that he wanted to solve.

He strolled over to stand beside her. 'Why didn't you apply for jobs in other parts of the world? Is there a reason you are reluctant to leave your village? A boyfriend perhaps?' He'd noted that she wasn't wearing a wedding ring, but she might have a long-term partner. It was an oddly unpalatable thought.

'No.' She gave him a wry look. 'Many of the people I was at school with have paired off and some have started families. The dating pool in Penash is very small, and anyway none of the local guys are interested in me.'

'I find that hard to believe.' He stared into her eyes that were sea green pools deep enough to drown in. As for her mouth, so lush and inviting. It was all Eirik could do to restrain himself from slanting his lips over hers and tasting her.

'It's true. No one wants to get involved with me because… I have crazy hair.' She ran her fingers through her riot of red curls and laughed, but it sounded strained, and he was sure she had been going to say something else.

'Your hair is incredible,' he murmured. Unable to resist, he lifted his hand and wound a silky curl around his finger. 'You are beautiful and intelligent. Courageous.' Eirik remembered the reason he had invited Arielle to meet him. One of the reasons, he mocked himself, conscious of the taut ache in his groin. 'Come inside,' he said softly. 'I have something for you.'

# CHAPTER THREE

'IT'S VERY KIND of you, but I can't accept this,' Arielle said firmly. For a second when she'd opened the slim box Eirik had handed her, and seen the sparkle of diamonds, her heart had missed a beat. The bracelet was exquisite. Even though she did not know much about proper jewellery—as opposed to the eco-friendly trinkets that she made—she could tell the bracelet was valuable.

'If you don't like the style, I will ask Gustav to arrange for an alternative to be sent to you. Perhaps you would prefer a necklace or diamond earrings?' He frowned when she shook her head. 'You risked your life to save mine, and the least I can do is gift you a small token to show my gratitude.'

'It's unnecessary.' Arielle's throat felt tight. 'I didn't know you were a prince when I realised that you were in trouble in the sea. I would have helped anyone, and I certainly did not expect to be rewarded.'

She replaced the lid on the box. The bracelet must have cost a fortune, but she felt cheapened that Eirik had turned her act of compassion into a commodity. Even worse, she felt a fool. He had flirted with her all evening, and when they had been on the balcony she'd thought for a heart-stopping moment that he was going to kiss her. She had wanted him to, she admitted. But the bracelet was a timely reminder that he wasn't interested in her, and his dinner invitation had simply been a polite gesture so that he could thank her for rescuing him.

He was a prince, and an inveterate womaniser by all accounts. No doubt he made every woman he met feel as though they'd stepped into the pages of a fairy tale. Arielle was annoyed with herself for being seduced by Eirik's charismatic personality. The truth was that she'd never met another man with his rampant sex appeal. Not even Jack, who she'd believed she was in love with, had made her feel so aware of her femininity.

But it was time for a reality check. She held out the box with the bracelet to Eirik. When he did not take it, she put it down on the table and said huskily, 'I should be going. It's late.'

Ten o'clock was hardly late, but she was impatient for the evening to be over. When she got home, she would hang her new dress in her wardrobe and look at it occasionally to remind herself that she had outgrown silly daydreams about handsome princes.

His frown deepened. 'I apologise if I have offended you. It was certainly not my intention.'

'You haven't,' she assured him in a too-bright voice. Her pulse quickened when he strolled towards her.

'Stay a little longer,' he said softly. 'I have enjoyed talking to you.'

There was temptation in the spicy scent of his aftershave mixed with something subtle but intrinsically male that made her stomach muscles clench. 'I really do have to leave. I've been working flat out to complete an order of recycled plastic jewellery for a London department store. It's a fantastic opportunity to showcase my products and publicise the Clean Sea campaign. I need to finish packing up the order tonight before it's collected by the courier tomorrow morning.'

'Your work is obviously important to you.' Was there a hint of pique in his cool voice? He probably did not get turned down by a woman very often, Arielle thought ruefully. Somehow it made her feel a bit better about her reaction to him. He was unfairly gorgeous, and she was not the first woman to be bowled over by him, nor would she be the last.

He picked up her shawl from the back of the chair and draped it around her shoulders. She felt the whisper of his warm breath on the side of her neck and her heart slammed against her ribcage.

'If I can't persuade you to change your mind I'll walk you down to the car,' he drawled.

Perversely she wished she hadn't decided to leave, but Eirik was striding over to the door and Arielle followed him out to the corridor. While the lift whisked them down to the lobby she avoided his curious gaze, but she was conscious of the prickling tension that filled the small space.

They left the hotel through the back door. Arielle held her breath when they passed the kitchens, but Danny Bray did not appear. She was surprised when Eirik led her across the staff car park to an old truck that looked the same as every other farm vehicle, with mud-spattered wheels and dents in the bodywork.

'The paparazzi who are camped outside the hotel do not take any notice of me when I drive past them in this,' he explained as he opened the passenger door and offered his hand to help her step up into the truck. He walked round to the driver's side, and Arielle's heart lurched when she realised that he intended to drive her home himself. She gave him directions to her cottage, and once they had left the main road, they were both silent while he concentrated on driving along the narrow lanes that wound up to the top of the cliffs.

'It's certainly remote,' he said when the truck rattled across the cattlegrid next to an old sign that said Rowse Farm. Arielle had been meaning to take the sign down, but few people visited her cottage. She tensed, wondering if Eirik had recognised the name of Cornwall's most notorious criminal. 'Do you keep livestock?' he asked.

'Not any more.'

The moon had disappeared behind clouds and the darkness was impenetrable. Eirik pulled up in the courtyard and switched off the engine. 'Do you ever feel spooked living out here on your own?'

'I'm not afraid of ghosts, if that's what you mean.'

Arielle was sure she'd switched the porch light on before she'd left, but the wiring in the cottage was old and the light bulbs had a habit of blowing.

Eirik got out of the truck and came round to open the passenger door. Once again, his nearness made her pulse quicken. Feeling flustered, she ignored his hand and jumped down. Her heel caught on a cobblestone, and she would have unbalanced if he hadn't caught her.

'Let me help you. Your shoes are not ideal for the terrain.'

It would be churlish to refuse. His old-fashioned chivalry was something she'd never experienced before, and butterflies fluttered in her stomach when he slipped his arm around her waist to support her over the uneven cobbles. In the dark porch Eirik used the torch on his phone so that Arielle was able to fit her key in the lock. She opened the front door that led directly into the living room and took a deep breath. 'Thank you for bringing me home.'

'It was my pleasure.' His face was all angles and planes in the shadows cast by the lamp just inside the door that she'd switched on. He did not move, and she could hardly close the door while he was standing there.

'Well, goodnight,' she murmured.

'You could invite me in for coffee.'

'I don't have coffee. I only buy tea because it's cheaper. Do you drink tea?'

'All the time.'

There was a gleam of mischief in his eyes as well

as something else that caused her heart to miss a beat. With a faint sigh, Arielle admitted to herself that she did not want the evening to end yet. 'In that case would you like to come in?'

'Thank you.' His smile made her think of a wolf, and she wondered if he viewed her as prey.

'Mind your head on the beams,' she warned as she ushered him into the living room.

He looked round the room. 'How old is this place?'

'It was built about two hundred years ago.' She had no idea if he thought the cottage was quaint or pokey. Since her father had been sent to prison, she'd covered the ancient sofa with brightly coloured throws and hung some of her mother's paintings on the walls to make the house feel more homely. 'The kitchen used to be a piggery and the bedrooms are in the attic where hay was once stored. You had better sit down,' she said, noticing that Eirik's head brushed against the low ceiling.

He dominated the small room, but it wasn't just his height and athletic build. He possessed a magnetism that would make him stand out in a crowd. 'I'll put the kettle on,' she said a little breathlessly. But she did not move. Her heart was thudding painfully hard. 'You're not a tea drinker, are you?'

'No.' He crossed the room in two strides and stared down at her. His mouth lifted at the corners, but his gaze was watchful and intense.

She gave a helpless shrug that turned into a shiver of excitement. 'Then why are you here?'

'You kissed me,' he drawled. 'I can't get the

memory of your lips pressed against mine out of my mind.' His husky accent made the tiny hairs on Arielle's skin stand on end.

She felt herself blush. 'It wasn't a kiss as such. You had almost drowned, and it was necessary for me to use mouth-to-mouth resuscitation on you.'

He laughed softly as he slid his hand beneath her chin and tilted her face up. 'Explain it to yourself that way if you want, but you kissed me, *skatta*, and I liked it, a lot. So much in fact that I think we should kiss properly. What do you say?'

Arielle tried to think of a flippant response, something that would ease the screaming sexual tension, but her mind was blank. The musk of male pheromones evoked a purely feminine reaction. Her breasts felt heavy and there was a dull ache between her legs. Shockingly, she imagined pressing her pelvis up against his and opening his zip while he shoved her dress out of the way and slipped his hand between her thighs. What was happening to her? She had never thrown herself at a man, but she had never met a man like Eirik.

His eyes glittered as he lowered his face towards hers, and she was powerless to stop him. His mouth was tantalisingly close. When his arms came around her, she allowed him to draw her against the solid wall of his chest. Her senses went wild as she was enveloped in his heat and his tantalising, male scent.

'You brought me back to life three nights ago,' he murmured. His breath whispered across her cheek. He grazed his lips over hers, once, twice, tasting her with leisurely sips that sent a quiver of anticipation through Arielle. Instinctively she knew that his light, almost playful kisses were a prelude to the passion building inexorably between them.

She moaned softly when he pushed his tongue between her lips, and he answered with a low groan, angling his mouth over hers and deepening the kiss until it was flagrantly erotic. Arielle melted against him, and reality faded.

*'Du er smukke,'* he murmured against her lips. He smiled at her puzzled expression. 'It's Fjernlandic for you are very beautiful.'

Where was her sanity when she needed it? 'I don't think…' *That this is a good idea.* But she did not finish her sentence for the good reason that he claimed her mouth in another breath-stealing kiss.

'Much better not to think. Instead, feel what you are doing to me.' He moved his hand down to her bottom and pulled her against his hard thighs. His groan of raw sexual need evoked a quiver of longing inside her. 'Why don't we continue this upstairs in your bedroom?' he asked thickly. 'I want to make love to you, and you want that too, don't you, my little mermaid?'

She did, heaven help her! Desire swept hot and urgent through her veins as Eirik's mouth sought hers once more. He kissed her with mounting hunger, and she responded with a wild abandon she'd never experienced before, a need that made her desperate to lead him upstairs to her bed.

Reality intruded as Arielle pictured her tiny bedroom with the narrow bed that she'd slept on since she was a little girl. There was still the mural on the wall of a princess in a castle that her mother had painted. The other bedroom along the landing was bigger than her room, but it was where her father had slept, and she never, ever went into that room.

She crashed back down to earth and stiffened in Eirik's arms. He lifted his mouth from hers and gave her a quizzical look.

'I think we should slow things down,' she said unsteadily. 'It's a big leap from dinner to bed.'

He released his breath slowly and dropped his hands down to his sides. 'Forgive my impatience, but I want you very badly and we only have tonight.'

Something cold and heavy replaced the fire he'd aroused in her. 'What happens after tonight?'

'I will return to Fjernland to accept the formal title of Hereditary Prince. The health of my father, the Sovereign Prince, is not good and, with the loss of my brother, it is my duty to prepare for the day when I will become monarch.' His gaze narrowed on her frozen expression. 'You and I can only ever be two shooting stars who briefly collide before continuing on our different trajectories.'

'In England we call it a one-night stand,' she said curtly. What a fool she was for thinking that Eirik was actually interested in her as a person when clearly all he wanted was sex.

He might not be so keen if she admitted that her sexual experience was limited to one disastrous relationship. Arielle remembered how Jack had fallen asleep immediately after sex, leaving her feeling unfulfilled. She'd assumed it was her fault their lovemaking had been disappointing. Often when she had visited Jack at his flat, he'd left a mountain of washing up and dirty laundry for her to do. He had treated her more like a servant than a girlfriend, but he had been her first and only proper relationship and she'd had low expectations as a result of growing up with her surly father, who had demanded that she kept the cottage clean and cooked his meals after her mother died when Arielle was a child.

One reason why she had been attracted to Jack was because she'd believed he did not know about her father. But he had admitted that he'd only been interested in her after he'd discovered that she was Gerran Rowse's daughter. Jack had been convinced that Arielle knew where her father had hidden money from his drug-dealing operation. Finding out that Jack had pretended to be in love with her had been another blow to her shaky self-confidence. Would she ever meet a man who genuinely wanted to be with her?

'I think you should leave,' she told Eirik stiffly.

His eyes were no longer the warm blue of summer skies. He gave her a haughty look that served as a reminder, if she had needed it, that they were not only from different countries, but they were worlds apart.

'We both got carried away,' he growled. 'There is nothing wrong with two consenting adults spending a pleasurable night together.' His jaw hardened. 'What did you expect?'

'That's my problem. I never expect anything, but maybe it's time I did.' Arielle bit down on her lower lip that felt slightly puffy from where he had kissed her with masterful passion. 'I really want you to go.' Before she made even more of an idiot of herself and burst into tears or, worse, asked him to stay.

He stared at her as if he couldn't believe she was turfing him out. It had probably never happened to him before. But she felt no sense of triumph in the thought, just a heaviness in her heart when without another word he strode across the room and opened the front door.

The breeze had picked up and above the rattle of a loose roof tile and the creaking branches of the hawthorn tree that was bowed by years of the punishing wind Arielle heard the barn door slam. Eirik stepped into the porch and his feet crunched on something on the floor. He bent down and picked up a shard of glass.

'I hadn't noticed when we arrived at the cottage, but it looks as if the light bulb was deliberately smashed.' He stooped again and, when he straightened up, Arielle saw he was holding a pebble that he'd found on the doormat.

The barn door clattered. 'I know I locked my studio,' she muttered. She grabbed a torch from the dresser, kicked off her high heels and slipped her feet into her wellington boots that were standing next to the front door.

'Wait here, and I'll go and check it out.' Eirik held out his hand for the torch. His expression told her she would be wasting her breath if she argued. She gave him the torch but followed him across the courtyard to the barn. Arielle sucked in a breath when she saw in the torch's gleam that the padlock on the door had been broken.

'Someone has been busy,' Eirik said grimly as he picked up an iron bar from the ground. 'This must have been used to break the lock.'

He pushed open the door and Arielle quickly found the light switch on the wall. The overhead strip light flickered and then became brighter.

'Oh, no.' Her brain took a few seconds to compute the carnage in front of her. The first things she saw were the ripped-open boxes that she'd packed, ready to be sent to the London department store. The numerous pieces of eco-friendly jewellery that she'd painstakingly created had been destroyed.

Tears filled her eyes as she looked around at the devastation in her studio. Her worktable had been upended and her collection of sea glass had been smashed and was scattered over the floor. She bent down and picked up two halves of a piece of pink glass that had obviously been hit with a hammer lying on the floor nearby. 'This was the first piece of sea glass in my collection. I found it when I was swimming in the sea with my mother,' she told Eirik. 'Pink sea glass is rare, and after Mum died I kept it because it reminded me of her.'

It was idiotic to cry over bits of broken glass, she told herself. Even worse was how much her silly treasures that she'd collected from the sea had meant to her. She had been hiding from real life in her studio, haunted by her past and afraid to face the future. 'Everything is ruined,' she choked out.

'Arielle…' The sympathy in Eirik's voice was too much to bear.

'Just…leave me alone.'

He took out his phone. 'I'll call the police.'

*'No.'* She hurried over to him, praying he hadn't noticed the graffiti that had been sprayed in red paint on the wall. *Blood on your hands.* It wasn't true, but some of the villagers believed that she had lied to protect her father when he had been charged with the murder of the young police constable, Josh Bray.

Arielle remembered Danny Bray's accusation that she had taken over running her father's drug-dealing business. Danny could not have known that the car with dark-tinted windows that had been seen outside her cottage had been driven by Prince Eirik's private secretary.

Eirik was frowning. 'Why don't you want to report the break-in and criminal damage done to your property to the police?'

'It will create more resentment,' she said in a low voice. 'Some of the local fishermen were angry when I supported a campaign for them to use more expensive biodegradable nets to reduce the amount of discarded plastic fishing equipment in the sea.' That much was true, although Arielle did not believe it was the reason her studio had been destroyed. 'I was planning to leave Penash anyway and now I have no reason to stay.'

* * *

'Where will you go?' Eirik frowned as Arielle avoided making eye contact with him. Something was going on that he did not understand. Her reluctance to involve the police about the break-in was odd, and he was not convinced by her explanation that her environmental campaigning had angered the villagers.

She hugged her arms around herself, and he sensed that her composure was on a knife-edge. 'I don't have any definite plans,' she admitted.

'Well, I suggest you make some quickly. In the meantime, is there somewhere you can go where you will be safe?' He thought of the smashed light bulb in the porch. 'Whoever destroyed your workshop might be planning to return and break into the cottage.'

'I'm sure that won't happen.' She bit her lip and Eirik was furious with himself when his gaze was drawn to her mouth, and he remembered how soft and moist her lips had felt beneath his. 'My best friend got married last year and moved to France with her husband. I'm not close to anyone else in the village. I'll do as you suggested and apply for a job abroad.'

'That will take time.' Eirik rubbed his hand over the stubble on his jaw. The idea that had come into his mind was admittedly not sensible. But his conscience would not allow him to leave Cornwall and abandon Arielle to the mercy of the thugs who had wrecked her studio. 'I have to fly back to Fjernland tomorrow and I want you to come with me.'

She stared at him. 'Why? You said that we are on different trajectories.'

Eirik glowered at her for reminding him of his crass behaviour. He'd come onto her like a teenager with an overload of hormones, and it wasn't his style at all. He blamed it on his libido, which had kicked into life after more than a year when he'd simply felt numb. Frustration was a nagging ache in his groin. But he had been honest with Arielle. He hadn't wanted her to think he could offer more, or indeed that he wanted more, than one night of mutual pleasure.

'Don't get the wrong idea. My offer to help you leave Penash has nothing to do with what happened, or didn't happen between us,' he said sardonically. 'I am indebted to you for saving my life. You want to pick up your career, and I can make it happen.'

Her green eyes flashed. 'You don't owe me anything and I am not your responsibility.'

His patience evaporated. 'Are you always so stubborn? You said you want to work in another country, and I happen to know that a temporary position to cover maternity leave will be available at the Fjernland Marine Research Institute. The director is a friend of mine. His wife is involved in a research project studying the effects of microplastic pollution in the oceans. Frida is expecting their first child soon and she intends to take several months off to be with the baby. I will give your CV to Valdemar. Obviously you would have to go through a proper interview process, but with your qualifications and experience I think you stand a good chance of being offered the job.'

'But I don't speak Fjernlandic,' Arielle said.

'It won't be a problem. All Fjernlanders are taught English at school from the age of five. Our national language is important, but we are a small principality and have to be able to communicate with the wider world.'

Eirik broke off when his phone rang. He cursed beneath his breath when he saw the name on the screen. Her Serene Highness, Princess Hulda—Eirik had been a toddler before he'd understood that the woman who had occasionally visited him in the palace nursery was his mother—had been short on sympathy and highly critical of his decision to take part in the AII race, which had ended disastrously for his new yacht and nearly cost him his life. A late-night call from the Princess was unexpected. 'I must take this,' Eirik excused himself to Arielle.

'Why are you still in England?' Princess Hulda did not waste her breath greeting him. 'Gustav informed me that you did not experience any ill effects from your yachting accident. It would have been nice if you had bothered to tell me yourself.'

Eirik refrained from reminding his mother that she had never shown any interest in his welfare until a little over a year ago, when he'd become the heir to the throne.

'I had assumed that you would return to Fjernland immediately. You need to be here.' The Princess spoke in her usual abrupt manner, but Eirik heard a rare note of emotion in her voice. 'Your father has been admitted to hospital with a suspected heart attack. If he dies, you will be the new monarch.'

# CHAPTER FOUR

'Was it a wise decision to invite Miss Tremain along?' Gustav murmured.

Eirik followed his private secretary's gaze across the aisle of the private jet to where Arielle was curled up on a leather recliner. She was fast asleep, which was hardly surprising as it was one o'clock in the morning. Eirik felt too wired up to sleep. 'I gather you do not think it was a wise decision,' he snapped.

'I simply thought that in light of the situation with your father's health you would not want any… distractions.'

'I spoke to my mother a few minutes ago. It appears that His Serene Highness did not have a heart attack and has been diagnosed with a condition called pericarditis, which is inflammation around the heart caused by a viral infection. Prince Otto is expected to make a full recovery.'

'I am very glad to hear that.' Gustav sat down when Eirik waved him to a chair. 'You must be extremely relieved.'

'Of course.' The news that his father's life was not

in danger felt as though a weight had been lifted from Eirik's shoulders. He was reprieved from becoming the ruling monarch of Fjernland, for the time being at least. More surprising had been the rush of emotion he'd felt. For most of his life he had not had a close relationship with Prince Otto, who had only been interested in Niels, the oldest son and heir to the throne. But recently Eirik had spent more time with his father while he'd prepared for when he would rule the principality.

A tentative rapprochement had developed between them, helped by the fact that Prince Otto had mellowed since he had battled cancer for two years. He had been given the all-clear, but this latest health scare had renewed Princess Hulda's determination that her husband should abdicate in favour of the surviving heir. However, Prince Otto had stated that he would not stand aside until Eirik was married.

'It is imperative that you choose a bride and marry her as quickly as it can be arranged.' Eirik replayed his latest phone conversation with his mother in his head. 'Baron Lundberg's daughter is ideal in every respect. She comes from one of the oldest aristocratic families in Fjernland, and she is charming, gracious and—'

'Chilly,' he had cut in.

'Don't be absurd.' Princess Hulda's voice had bristled with impatience. 'What do you even mean?'

'It doesn't matter,' he'd murmured as he'd pictured Ida's cool, blonde beauty.

'If you have decided that you do not want Ida

Lundberg to be your Princess Consort there are plenty of other suitable candidates on my list.'

'Seriously, you have a list?'

'Of course I have a list. You have had over a year to choose a wife, but you have made no effort to do that one simple thing.' The Princess's displeasure had been obvious. 'It would not have been necessary if your brother had lived,' she had reminded Eirik. 'Niels would have married Princess Catalina and ascended the throne on your father's abdication.'

*If only you hadn't suggested the skiing trip.*

His mother's unspoken accusation had evoked a familiar, eviscerating guilt in Eirik's gut.

The truth was that Ida Lundberg would make him a perfect wife and she had made it clear when they had met at society events in the past year that she was keen to be the Princess Consort. Keener on the title than on having him as her husband, Eirik suspected cynically. Ida was renowned in European high society for her elegance and sophistication. It was impossible to imagine her swimming in a wild sea wearing a mermaid's tail.

His gaze was drawn by some invisible force to Arielle. Her riotous red curls were constrained in a thick braid. Before leaving the cottage in Cornwall she had changed out of her sexy black dress into jeans and a fine wool jumper that moulded her firm breasts. Her dark green jumper was the same colour as her eyes, which right now were hidden behind her closed eyelids. Her long auburn eyelashes were fanned on her softly flushed cheeks and beneath her left eye was a small, barely noticeable scar.

Eirik wanted to know how she had got the scar. Hell, he wanted to know everything about her. That should have set an alarm bell ringing. He enjoyed women's company in the bedroom, but he never allowed himself to be pinned down in a relationship. He was perplexed by his desperate need to cover Arielle's lush red lips with his mouth and lose himself in the unguarded sensuality of her kiss. It was that word *need* that troubled him.

His mind flew back to when they had discovered that Arielle's studio had been ransacked. He had tried to persuade her to take the job opportunity in Fjernland, but then he'd received the phone call from his mother.

'Has something happened?' Arielle had been sweeping up the broken glass on the floor. She'd leaned the broom against the wall and hurried over to him. 'You look as if you have received bad news.'

'My father has collapsed, and I must return to Fjernland tonight.'

'How awful. I'm so sorry.' She had put her hand on his arm, and the gentle expression in her sea green eyes had tugged on something inside Eirik. Arielle's livelihood had been destroyed, but she had been more concerned for him, and her compassion had shaken him.

'I need you to come with me,' he'd blurted out. He did not know where the words had come from. For as long as he could remember he had only cared about his brother. Since Niels had gone, the warm place in Eirik's heart where his brother had resided had frozen over. Arielle had looked as shocked as Eirik had felt.

'You saved my life and now it is my turn to help you,' he'd told her. He had assured himself that obviously it was what he had meant. 'I don't feel responsible for you,' he'd insisted when he'd seen the storm brewing in her eyes. 'I will introduce you to the head of Fjernland's Marine Research Institute, and it will be for Valdemar to decide whether to offer you a job, and for you to accept or not. The likelihood is that you and I will not meet again when I am busy with royal duties.'

It was the truth, Eirik brooded as his mind returned to the present. The minute the plane landed in Fjernland his life would no longer be his own. He would go straight to the hospital to visit his father and then to the palace, where he might manage to snatch a couple of hours' sleep before a day of meetings with royal advisors and government ministers in his capacity as the Reigning Sovereign's deputy. He certainly would not have time to be distracted by a flame-haired siren.

Beside him Gustav cleared his throat. 'I was wondering what plans you have made for Miss Tremain when we arrive in Fjernland. Might I suggest that it would not be a good idea for you to be seen with her in public? No doubt there will be news reporters outside the hospital and at Sejrrig Palace.'

The private secretary was right. The information

that Prince Otto was in hospital had been leaked to the press and it was likely that there would also be paparazzi photographers outside the building where Eirik owned a penthouse apartment. Not that he had considered taking Arielle there. Tempting though she was, he must put duty before his personal pleasure from now on. But she would have to stay somewhere until he could arrange for her to have an interview at the marine research institute. He could send her to a hotel, but his conscience pricked that it would be unfair to abandon her in a strange country.

He needed to take Arielle somewhere where she would not attract the attention of the press or cause gossip among the palace staff. A place that was out of the way, and with someone whose discretion he could rely on.

Catalina was the obvious solution. She understood him better than anyone and they had forged a strong bond through their shared grief for Niels. Eirik sent a text message on his phone. When he glanced at his private secretary, he saw that Gustav's head had drooped and his chin was resting on his chest.

He had been a surly sixteen-year-old when Gustav had been appointed as his equerry. Over the years the older man had become a loyal and trusted friend, and in many ways he had been a better father than Eirik's own father. He stood up and pressed the control panel to recline Gustav's chair before covering him with a blanket.

He looked over at Arielle and his heart banged against his ribs as his eyes met her sea green gaze.

She stretched her arms above her head, and he felt a certain part of his anatomy jerk to attention when her jumper rose up to reveal a strip of bare stomach above the waistband of her jeans.

*Faen!* Eirik cursed beneath his breath. He could not remember ever being so fiercely attracted to a woman. After Niels had died, he had felt bereft, and he'd lost interest in everything, including sex. Arielle had reignited his urges, but, for a man who had always been in control of himself, it was disconcerting to find that his body had a will of its own.

'We will arrive in Fjernland in just over an hour,' he informed her in a cool voice that he hoped disguised the fire raging inside him.

She gave a tiny yawn. 'I don't think Gustav approves of me.'

'Possibly he doesn't. He thinks you could be trouble.'

Her eyes widened. 'What do you mean?'

'Gustav knows that I find you desirable.' Eirik decided that if he acknowledged the problem he would be able to deal with his inconvenient attraction and dismiss it.

Colour ran along Arielle's high cheekbones. 'You do?'

'Don't pretend you are unaware of what you do to me. We both feel an awareness, chemistry, whatever you want to call it.'

She nibbled her lower lip but did not deny the truth of his statement.

'Gustav's concern is unnecessary,' Eirik assured

Arielle. 'Our stars briefly orbited each other, but from now on our lives are set on different paths. You want to kickstart your career and I will become the ruling sovereign of my country.'

But first there was the matter of his marriage, which would happen sooner rather than later if his mother had her way.

Arielle leaned back in her seat and closed her eyes again, but she had napped for a couple of hours and no longer felt sleepy. When she had boarded the private jet with Eirik, she'd been overwhelmed by tiredness, partly as a result of the shock of discovering that her studio had been destroyed. She was sure that Danny Bray had been responsible, but if she'd reported the break-in to the police, as Eirik had wanted her to do, there had been a chance that he would have learned of her father's crimes.

Through her half-closed eyelashes she studied the Prince, who was sprawled in a chair on the opposite side of the plane. He had opened his laptop and took no further notice of her. Eirik was an enigma, Arielle thought ruefully. In one breath he'd admitted that he desired her, but he'd gone on to say that when they arrived in Fjernland he would be busy with his royal duties, and they were unlikely to meet again. Clearly he would not find it difficult to dismiss her from his mind, but she doubted she would forget him so easily. It was silly to feel hurt that Eirik planned to abandon her once he had introduced her to the head of the marine research institute, but it emphasised that all he'd wanted was to have sex with her for one night.

Arielle remembered that Eirik had said he wanted to help her leave Cornwall because he felt indebted to her for saving him when his yacht had sunk in the storm. It was hard to believe that she had finally left the cottage in Penash where she had felt trapped by her father's control over her, and, after he had been sent to prison, by her lack of confidence. She felt a mixture of trepidation and excitement as she tried to imagine herself living and working in Fjernland.

The only other time she had been abroad was when she'd gone to France for her best friend's wedding. Flora had been in Arielle's class at school and had also been bullied by some of the other girls because her mother had a reputation in the village for having numerous lovers. Now Flora was happily married to Jean-Luc, who owned a vineyard in Provence. Arielle was glad for her friend, and a little envious. Would she ever meet a man who would love and cherish her? She had often wondered if her mother had loved her father when she had married him. It was hard to imagine that Gerran had ever been kind or loving. Falling in love required a leap of faith, and Arielle's childhood had left her with trust issues. It was odd then, she thought with a jolt, that she trusted Eirik enough to leave Cornwall to start a new life in his country.

She must have dozed, and she woke to the sound of her name. Eirik was leaning over her and dropped his hand from her shoulder when she stirred. Her gaze meshed with his and she recognised the flare of sexual interest in his bright blue eyes before he straightened up abruptly as if he'd felt as burned by their momentary closeness as she did.

'We are about to land,' he told her. 'I must go to the hospital to see my father, but first I'll take you to stay with a friend of mine for the remainder of the night.'

'I can go to a hotel rather than disturb your friend.'

'Catalina is expecting you. Fasten your seat belt,' he instructed, giving her no chance to ask further questions as he returned to his seat in preparation for the landing.

A car was waiting for them at the side of the runway. Eirik had explained that Fjernland's main airport was near the capital city Ved Floden, but they had come to a private airfield. He ushered Arielle into the back of the car and slid in beside her. Gustav got into the front, next to the driver. Arielle felt a definite vibe of disapproval from Eirik's private secretary. She stared out of the window, but in the darkness she could not make out much, especially when the road wound through thick woodland. Eventually they came to a clearing where there was a large house. The chauffeur opened the door and she followed Eirik across the driveway to the front door, which was opened by a butler.

As they stepped inside, a woman walked towards them. She was exotically beautiful, with long, lustrous black hair. She carried herself with a curiously regal bearing and her kaftan-style dress whispered around her ankles so that she appeared to glide across the floor. The many gold bangles on her wrists gleamed in the light from the chandelier.

*'Caro,'* she greeted Eirik warmly and kissed him on both cheeks. 'It is good to see you.'

'Lina,' he murmured softly. 'I did not expect you to wait up.'

The woman gave a heavy sigh. 'You know how it is. I do not sleep well.'

'This is Arielle Tremain.' Eirik turned to Arielle. 'May I introduce Princess Catalina of San Sabinus?'

*Princess!* Arielle had a vague idea that San Sabinus was a principality somewhere off the coast of southern Italy. She remembered her manners and quickly curtseyed to the Princess.

Princess Catalina's faint smile did not reach her eyes. 'Gerado will show you to your room, Miss Tremain.'

The butler took Arielle's bag that Eirik had carried from the car. She hesitated and her heart sank as she wondered if this was the last time she would see him. She wanted to ask him about his friendship with the beautiful princess.

'I'll be in contact tomorrow to let you know about your interview at the marine research institute.' Eirik's handsome face showed no emotion, and his dismissive tone suggested that he had quashed the spark of desire he'd felt for her.

'Thank you.' Arielle kept her tone as cool as his had been. As she followed the butler across the entrance hall, she heard Princess Catalina speak to Eirik.

'Is there any news on your father?'

'His condition is not as serious as was first thought.'

'Thank God you are spared another tragedy, *caro*.' There was raw emotion in the Princess's voice.

The following morning, when Arielle woke up, she was disorientated for a few moments before she remembered where she was. It had been a disturbed night, and she did not function well without a solid eight hours of sleep. A shower revived her somewhat. She had thrown clean underwear and a few other essentials into an overnight bag before she'd left the cottage with Eirik. After pulling on jeans and sweater, she ventured out of her room and went downstairs.

The house was large and rather gloomy, surrounded by thick forest that blocked the light coming through the windows. In the distance Arielle saw the gleam of water. The sound of someone weeping drew her towards the dining room. The table was laid for breakfast, but Princess Catalina was not eating. She had buried her face in her hands and her sobs were heart-wrenching.

Arielle was torn between the need to respect the Princess's privacy and a deep sense of compassion. 'Forgive me for intruding,' she murmured as she stepped into the room. 'Is there anything I can do to help you?'

'I am afraid not.' Princess Catalina lowered her

hands from her face. Her eyes were red and puffy from crying. She indicated that Arielle should sit down. 'So you are the mermaid. Eirik told me how you saved his life,' she explained, noticing Arielle's start of surprise.

'He told me that you are a close friend of his,' she said stiffly.

The Princess nodded. 'I was engaged to Eirik's brother, Prince Niels.'

Of course. Arielle remembered why Princess Catalina's name had seemed familiar. When Prince Niels had been killed just over a year ago, it had been reported that his fiancée was distraught. 'I'm so sorry.'

'Eirik loved his brother as deeply as I adored Niels. Since the accident we have grieved together.' Catalina sighed. 'Both our lives have been changed for ever. I would have become the Princess Consort on my marriage to Niels, who was to have become the Reigning Sovereign. Prince Otto wishes to abdicate and pass the responsibilities of being the monarch to his remaining son, but he is insistent that Eirik must choose a bride and marry to produce an heir.'

A heavy weight dropped into the pit of Arielle's stomach. 'Does Eirik have someone in mind?' she asked, trying to sound casual, but she saw Princess Catalina give her a speculative look.

'It is expected that he will soon make a formal announcement of his betrothal to the daughter of Fjernland's second most important family.

Ida Lundberg is entirely suitable to be the Princess Consort, and Eirik will be involved with the preparations for a royal wedding.'

The Princess rose to her feet and gathered her silk robe around her. 'Please sit and enjoy your breakfast,' she said when Arielle made to stand up. 'I understand that Eirik's staff packed up your belongings at your house in England and your luggage arrived early this morning. If you want to swim, the lake is heated by geothermal activity and I am told it is as warm as a bath, although I have not swum in it myself.'

Princess Catalina walked across the room and paused in the doorway. 'One more thing. I do not recommend that you fall in love with the Prince. He has assured his parents that he will devote himself to duty and the monarchy, and there will be no room in his life for…distractions.'

Arielle was reeling from the news that Eirik intended to marry. No wonder he had said he could only spend one night with her when he'd kissed her at the cottage, she thought dismally. She felt her face grow warm. 'I definitely won't fall for him,' she said staunchly. But she couldn't promise not to boil Eirik in oil if she got the chance.

Princess Catalina studied her for a few moments. 'Love is the greatest beauty and tragedy of our lives,' she told Arielle softly before she swept out of the room.

The mountains in the distance were snow-capped, and this far north of the equator the spring sunshine did not have much heat, but the temperature of the geothermal lake was warm enough for Arielle to swim without a wetsuit. Swimming was usually her stress release. The water was crystal clear, and she dived deep, propelled by her monofin tail that she'd found with the rest of her luggage. Rising to the surface again, she floated on her back and stared up at the cloudless sky.

When she had left Cornwall last night, she'd felt excited about coming to Fjernland. But today she was apprehensive about her future in a strange country where she had only a vague suggestion of a possible job, and she did not know anyone apart from the Prince, who had made it clear he would not have any time for her. For once in her life, she had acted impulsively, but now she was beset by doubts.

Although it was foolish, she was disappointed that there was no chance of the attraction between her and Eirik developing into…what? Arielle asked herself. He had been honest with her and said they could not have more than a one-night stand. It was entirely her fault that her heart had longed for a fairy-tale romance with a handsome prince. But the stark reality was that Eirik must marry, and he certainly would not choose a woman with her background to be his princess. Arielle had searched on the Internet for information about Eirik's possible future wife and discovered that the houses of Sorensen and Lundberg could be traced back to when Viking warriors had fought bloody battles to claim independence for Fjernland. And then there was Ida herself. Photographs showed her to be classically beautiful and the epitome of elegance and refinement. She was highly regarded in court circles and would be a popular choice with the Fjernlandic people when Eirik made her his Princess Consort.

So why had he flirted with her? Arielle knew the answer. He had shown her a glimpse of heaven when he'd held her in his arms, and she had convinced herself that there had been tenderness in his kiss. But all Eirik had wanted was to scratch an itch. She was glad she hadn't succumbed to his potent charm. At her cottage in Cornwall it had been Eirik's last night of freedom before returning to Fjernland and the life of duty that awaited him, and presumably he had decided that she would be a convenient bed-mate. It was ridiculous how badly the truth hurt. *She* was ridiculous. Angry with herself for being such a fool, Arielle ducked beneath the surface and swam to the far end of the lake.

When she looked back towards the house, she saw a boat being rowed across the lake. The bright sunshine turned Eirik into a gilded god, and he had the physique of a top athlete as he powered the oars through the water. Arielle's pulse quickened. She had not expected to see him again and she'd assumed he would be busy with royal duties. He had told her on the plane that Prince Otto hadn't suffered a heart attack but would need time to recover from an illness.

Reluctant to face Eirik while her emotions were in turmoil, Arielle dived down to the bottom of the lake and hoped he would row back to the shore. Looking up through the clear water, she could see the dark shape of the underside of the boat. Eventually a need for air meant she had to swim to the surface.

'There you are,' he said softly when he saw her. His smile drove the breath that she'd just snatched into her lungs out again in a whoosh. He was *so* handsome and, despite herself, Arielle felt her treacherous body respond to his potency.

'Aren't you a bit overdressed for boating?' she murmured, eyeing his exquisitely tailored three-piece suit. He had taken the jacket off and draped it over the seat in the boat. His shirt sleeves were rolled up to his elbows and his blue silk waistcoat emphasised the broadness of his chest.

'I had breakfast with the Foreign Minister, and I was in meetings for the rest of the morning. There are a lot of arrangements to be made for a big event that will take place soon.'

He must mean his wedding. Arielle hated how her heart dropped into the pit of her stomach. Eirik meant nothing to her, she reminded herself. He leaned over the side of the boat and stretched out his hand to trace the edge of her sparkly green bikini top. She held her breath when his knuckles brushed against the slopes of her breasts, above the triangles of stretchy material. 'You are certainly not overdressed,' he said roughly. 'You are a siren, and you have cast a spell on me, *skatta*. I can't stop thinking about you.'

Time stopped, and her foolish heart leapt. She

tilted her face up and her eyes locked with his brilliant blue gaze. Eirik's lips were centimetres away from hers and Arielle shivered in anticipation of his kiss. A cloud blotted out the warmth of the sun, and she shivered again as cold disgust replaced the heat in her veins. Eirik was as good as engaged to be married, and in Arielle's opinion he had no right to say that he could not stop thinking about her, much less to be about to kiss her. She snatched her mouth away from the temptation of his and, with a flick of her monofin tail, dived beneath the boat and surfaced again on the other side.

He grinned. 'Give me a minute to strip off and I'll join you in the water.'

'What a good idea.' She was furious with him and with herself for being so fiercely attracted to him. Arielle told herself that she deserved better than to be a brief distraction for a prince before he settled to married life. She placed her hands on the edge of the boat and used all her strength to pull down, just as Eirik stood up and started to undo the belt on his trousers. The boat rocked dangerously.

'Hey, what are you doing?' He tried to balance himself, but she held onto the gunwale and gave a hard, downwards tug. Her tail gave her extra momentum, and as the boat tipped over Eirik was catapulted into the lake. Arielle heard him swear before there was a splash. She did not wait around and started to swim towards the shore, kicking her tail to propel herself in a sinuous motion through the water.

The stony beach where she had left her clothes was farther away than she'd realised. She was breathing hard by the time she reached the shallows. When she glanced over her shoulder, she panicked when she saw that Eirik had hauled himself back into the boat and was rowing after her.

The monofin had allowed Arielle to swim fast, but now she was stranded on the beach. She frantically attempted to wriggle out of the mermaid costume that had moulded itself to her lower body. In normal circumstances she could slip the tail on and off in a few minutes, but she was flustered and sweating. She cursed as she tried to tug the clingy material over her hips while keeping an eye on the boat as it came nearer.

'Goddammit!' Her situation was laughably ridiculous, but Eirik's furious expression warned her that he was not amused.

He jumped out of the boat and dragged it onto the pebbles. 'What the hell did you do that for? Thanks to your juvenile actions, my suit is ruined, and my jacket is at the bottom of the lake with my credit cards and phone.'

His trousers were soaked and plastered to his hard thighs. Through his wet shirt clinging to his chest Arielle could see the outline of his impressive pectoral muscles. Her heart missed a beat when he unfastened the buttons and slipped his shirt off so that he could ring the water out of it. She tore her gaze from his tanned chest covered with whorls of golden hairs and vainly tried to shift herself across the stones, but she was hampered by her tail.

Eirik gave a triumphant laugh. 'I've heard of a fish out of water, but never a mermaid. You are well and truly trapped, my beauty.'

# CHAPTER FIVE

ARIELLE MADE ANOTHER attempt to shuffle away from Eirik, but it was futile when the lower half of her body was tightly wrapped in a tube of silicone rubber—recycled of course.

'Not so fast,' he mocked her. He dropped to his knees and straddled her with his thighs on either side of her body. She caught her breath when she realised that the angry gleam in his eyes was mixed with something more dangerous. The air around them simmered with sexual tension, but she was determined to resist her treacherous body's desire for him.

'Leave me alone.' She pushed against his chest, but he captured her wrists in his hands and held them above her head.

'I thought the point of the game was for me to chase, and for you to capitulate, *skatta*.'

'We are not playing a game.' To her horror, the idea of capitulating to Eirik's sensual demands made her breathing quicken. 'I don't know what *skatta* means,' she muttered, hoping to distract his attention from the swift rise and fall of her breasts.

He shrugged. 'In English I suppose it means honey or sweetheart.' His eyes were still on her breasts and Arielle was mortified when she felt her nipples swell, and she knew the hard points must be visible through her bikini top.

'I am not your sweetheart. How could you put me in such a humiliating position? I don't mean the one I'm in now,' she snapped when his brows rose. She was pinned beneath him and totally at his mercy.

She bit her lip. 'You should not have brought me here to Princess Catalina's house. I feel awkward that I have invaded her privacy while she is grieving for her fiancé, your brother, Niels.'

Eirik lifted himself off Arielle and sat beside her on the pebbles. He raked his hand through his wet hair. 'I did not want to abandon you at a hotel, and it was only for last night. I rushed through my meetings this morning so I could come to collect you and take you to your interview with the director of the marine institute.'

He sighed heavily. 'Catalina was devastated when Niels was killed a week before their wedding, and she could not bear to return to San Sabinus. Instead, she came here to the holiday home they had bought as a place to escape to, away from the spotlight of royal life. In the past year she and I have grown close. Lina would have been my sister-in-law and she loved Niels as much as I did,' he said gruffly.

Arielle had finally managed to peel her mermaid's tail down her legs and slipped her feet out of the moulded foot compartment of the monofin. Beneath the costume she was wearing tiny bikini bottoms. She flushed when Eirik roved his bold gaze over her skimpily clad figure. The warmth of feminine arousal between her legs made her despise her body for its weakness for him.

'Princess Catalina told me that you are going to marry an aristocratic woman, Ida Lundberg.' She glared at Eirik. 'You had no right to kiss me and ask me to sleep with you when you had already promised to make another woman your bride.'

He frowned. 'You're wrong—'

'Don't tell me I'm wrong.' Arielle's temper blazed. She had spent most of her life feeling voiceless, too afraid of her father to speak out against him. She hadn't complained when Jack had treated her badly because she'd felt worthless and been grateful that he was her boyfriend.

She stood up and marched over to where she had left her clothes, trying not to wince as the pebbles dug into the soles of her feet. She thrust one leg into her jeans and hopped inelegantly while she stepped into the other leg. Her heart crashed into her ribs when she turned her head and discovered that Eirik had followed her up the beach. His close proximity and raw masculinity made her feel dizzy.

She yanked her jeans up her legs with such force that the denim scraped over her thighs. 'You made a fool of me when you kissed me knowing that you have a fiancée.'

'I am not engaged to Ida Lundberg,' he bit out.

'I haven't promised her or any other woman that I will marry them.'

'But Princess Catalina said that everyone expects you will formally announce your betrothal to Ida. And you told me that you had spent this morning planning a big event. I assumed you meant your wedding.' Arielle searched Eirik's face for any signs that he had lied. He held her gaze steadily, and she was the first to break eye contact.

He exhaled heavily. 'I am under pressure to marry a woman from an aristocratic background who will be my Princess Consort when I become ruler of Fjernland. My mother has let it be known publicly that she believes Ida Lundberg is the ideal candidate for the role, but I have not formally discussed the matter with Ida.'

*Yet.* Arielle mentally filled in the space when Eirik hesitated. She had always known he was out of her league, she reminded herself. But she felt a little happier knowing that, when he'd kissed her, he hadn't been cheating on a woman who had hopes of marrying him.

He stepped closer to her and took her sweater, which she was clutching tightly as if it were a security blanket, out of her fingers. 'For now, I am a bachelor and free to kiss whoever I desire,' he drawled.

Did he mean that he desired her? The sun was in her eyes, and she could not read his expression, but she hadn't imagined the hunger that thickened his voice. A shiver of longing ran through her. She did not move and could barely breathe as he lowered his face towards hers.

'Tell me you don't feel the same way and I'll end this madness now,' he said rawly.

The sensible thing would be to walk away from him. But Arielle did not want to be sensible. She could not lie and so she said nothing. Her lips parted in an unconscious invitation and Eirik's eyes narrowed to gleaming slits as he slanted his mouth over hers. He made her wait a fraction longer, and she trembled, every nerve ending on her body so acutely aware of him that it *hurt*.

She heard a low moan and realised as he closed the tiny gap between their mouths that the husky plea had come from her. But then her mind went blank as Eirik claimed her lips in a kiss that was thrillingly possessive. It was different from when he'd kissed her at the cottage. Then he had taken his time and teased her with light, almost playful caresses. But now there was nothing teasing in the way he ground his mouth down on hers and pushed his tongue between her lips.

Now there was heat and flame as her body caught light. The stubble on his jaw felt abrasive against her cheek when he kissed his way up to the sensitive place behind her ear before he nipped her earlobe with his teeth. She pressed herself closer to him and felt the play of hard muscles beneath her palms when she placed her hands on his chest. His skin felt like satin, overlaid with soft hairs that were springy beneath her fingertips.

Eirik tightened his arm around her waist and pushed his other hand between their bodies to cup her breast. He rubbed his thumb over her nipple and sensation shivered through her. The thin material of her bikini was a frustrating barrier. She wanted his hands on her naked skin and she must have spoken out loud because he laughed softly and brought his other hand up her back to release the clasp on her bikini top.

It fell away and he closed his fingers around her bare breast, playing with her nipple and making her gasp with pleasure. Reality faded, and Arielle was aware of nothing but this golden prince who seemed to understand her body better than she did herself. He seemed to know of the insistent ache between her thighs and clamped his hand on her bottom, hauling her against him so that her pelvis was flush to his and her bones turned to liquid when she felt the hard proof of his arousal.

It had been a mistake to kiss Arielle. Eirik knew it the moment his lips met hers, but the taste of her was more intoxicating than a fine wine and he wanted more. She was so damned responsive, pressing herself up against him and winding her arms around his neck as she opened her mouth beneath his and held nothing back.

Her soft breast filled his palm, and he liked the way she moaned when he rolled her nipple between his thumb and forefinger. He liked it way too much. It was as if he had never done this before. He felt as excited as a teenager exploring a woman's body for the first time. But Eirik had done a lot of exploring and he'd slept with more women than he could remember. This was different, this insane need to strip Arielle naked and possess her with fast, hard strokes.

Where could he do it? Here? He tore his mouth from hers and glanced around him. The lake was some distance from the house, and they were unlikely to be disturbed by Princess Catalina or the household staff. But the pebbly beach would be an uncomfortable place to have sex. He thought of carrying Arielle up to the grassy bank and making love to her there. But he did not have a condom, and she might not use any sort of contraceptive.

Finally, Eirik's brain kicked into gear. He could not risk having unprotected sex with Arielle. And definitely not in a place that had been special to his brother. He remembered when he and Niels had sat beside the lake and talked of the future.

'I will bring my children here and teach them to swim. Catalina and I are planning to try for a baby as soon as we are married,' Niels had said.

'You need an heir.' Eirik had thanked his lucky stars that he was not the future Sovereign and did not have to bother with marriage or babies.

'I want a baby with Lina because I love her more than I knew it was possible to love someone. Wait until it happens to you,' Niels had told Eirik with a smile. 'Love creeps up on you when you are not expecting it, and then—*pow*!'

But Niels's life had been obliterated by an avalanche and the crown would pass to Prince Otto's second-born son. The second-best son, Eirik thought grimly. It was how his parents had always made him feel. He had told himself he didn't care and had built a life and career away from the stifling royal court. He had made a fortune and was a multimillionaire in his own right. That achievement at least had impressed his father. But now his future would be very different from the freedom and independence he had once enjoyed.

He had begun the process of selling his business, Sorensen Yachts,, and he was preparing to devote his life to duty. It was up to him to prove he was worthy of the role that should have been his brother's. So what was he doing, instigating casual sex with a beautiful siren who could never be his Princess Consort? Arielle would lure him to his doom unless he resisted her sensual witchery.

Eirik stared into her sea green eyes and knew for sure that she had cast a spell on him when she reached up and pressed her lips to his. Her sweet breath filled his mouth and he kissed her because he simply could not stop himself. She was heat and flame and he was burning up. He had never felt so out of control.

The sobering thought made him wrench his mouth from hers and set her away from him. Her hair was drying into titian curls and her bare breasts were creamy globes tipped with dusky rose nipples that he ached to suck on.

'This can't lead anywhere,' he told Arielle. His voice rasped in his throat.

'I don't care.' Her eyes were glazed and there was a hectic flush on her cheeks. She put her hands on his chest and he wondered if she could feel the erratic thud of his heart. 'I know that our lives are on different paths, but I want this one time with you before we go our separate ways. I want you to teach me everything, Eirik.'

He understood then just how much of a threat she was. The temptation to pull her back into his arms and take what she was offering was an insistent drumbeat in his blood. His arousal was uncomfortably hard. But an alarm bell rang inside his head.

'Teach you? Are you saying that you are a virgin?' He must have sounded as appalled as he felt.

Arielle bit her lip. 'No, of course I'm not. I had a boyfriend for a while. Not a very nice one as it happens. It…sex…wasn't great, and, if you must know, he didn't…satisfy me.'

*Faen!* Eirik swore silently. Arielle's face was scarlet. Her vulnerability was the most dangerous thing of all. He suspected that, for her, sex and emotions were inextricably linked. But he did not do emotions.

He captured her hands and pulled them away from his chest before he stepped back from her. 'This was a mistake.' He forced himself to sound coolly dismissive, despite the thunderous desire still pounding inside him. He could not risk having sex with Arielle and for her to think that he might develop feelings for her. There was no chance of that happening.

Impossibly her face turned even redder, and the blush spread down her throat and décolletage. Eirik wondered if her pale breasts would flush so prettily pink with the heat of sexual desire. But he would never find out.

'You started this,' she said in a low voice that held the suspicion of tears.

'And now I'm finishing it.' He stooped to pick up her jumper and held it out to her. 'Get dressed.' Eirik hoped he would feel more in control of himself when he was not faced with the tantalising sight of Arielle's naked breasts.

'I told you the truth when I said I have not promised marriage to any woman. But the event I have been involved in organising is a masquerade ball, which will take place two weeks from now, at my official residence, the Winter Palace. The ball is to celebrate my birthday.' He grimaced. 'My mother has decided that it is an ideal opportunity to invite every woman who she deems suitable to be my future Princess Consort, and there is an expectation that I will announce I have chosen my bride.'

'You make it sound so businesslike. How can you be sure you will fall in love with a woman who has your mother's approval?'

'I have no intention of falling in love. Nor do I want a wife who might fall in love with me. In that respect Ida Lundberg is ideal. Since childhood, her goal has been to become the Princess Consort. Her father hoped she would marry my brother, but Niels met Princess Catalina and it was love at first sight.

Now Baron Lundberg sees another opportunity to link our two families.'

'How romantic,' Arielle said drily. 'Why is your mother in such a rush for you to get married?'

'Two years ago, my father was diagnosed with a malignant tumour. While he underwent treatment, he gave in to my mother's pleas for him to abdicate and allow Niels to become ruler of Fjernland with Princess Catalina as Consort after their wedding. Obviously that did not happen,' Eirik said gruffly. 'Prince Otto has made a full recovery from cancer, but my mother is desperate for him to retire from public life. My father has agreed to stand down in favour of me, but only when I have a wife who will hopefully give me an heir.'

Eirik looked away from Arielle's wide-eyed stare. He was royalty and this was how these things were arranged. That was what he had been taught. Love played no part in the begetting of heirs who would ensure the House of Sorensen's bloodline as rulers of the principality that few people outside Fjernland had heard of.

By lucky chance his brother had fallen in love with a princess, who would have been his bride. But Eirik knew there was a dark side to love. Jealousy, despair, rejection; he understood that his mother had suffered those things in her marriage to his father, and he had experienced them himself when he'd been hurt by his parents' indifference before he had learned to detach from his emotions.

He glanced at his watch. 'We should get back.' He

waited while Arielle rolled up her mermaid's tail, and she followed him as he strode up the beach. The path through the woods was just wide enough for them to walk side by side. The tall trees all around made the air feel close, or perhaps it was his intense awareness of the woman beside him that constricted his lungs.

'My mother was in her early twenties when she fell in love with my father. Prince Otto was nearly forty and enjoyed a playboy lifestyle before and after they were married.'

Eirik was aware of the surprised look Arielle gave him. He had no idea why he was telling her about his dysfunctional family. 'My parents were civil towards each other, but I never saw affection between them. I was about thirteen when I heard a rumour circulating at the palace that Prince Otto's dalliance with a kitchen maid was not his first affair, nor likely to be his last.' He shrugged. 'My father married because he needed a son, and Princess Hulda duly provided an heir and a spare. She showered her love that her husband had spurned on my brother.'

'What about you? Surely your mother loved you as much as your brother.'

'I was only ever an afterthought, an insurance policy if something happened to Niels. I'm not telling you this because I want sympathy,' he growled. 'I am my father's son, and for me marriage is an unavoidable duty. I cannot promise the woman I will marry love and romance. All I can offer is a crown.'

'You still haven't explained the urgency for you to get married.'

'My mother nursed my father when he had cancer, and after thirty-six years of marriage Prince Otto fell in love with his wife. Finally, my mother has what she has always wanted—her husband's full attention. But my father will not retire from royal duties until I marry.'

The weight of his guilt and his mother's expectations were a burden that Eirik would always carry. 'I can't deny my mother her chance of happiness with my father in retirement. Niels would have become the Reigning Sovereign a year ago. It's my fault that my brother died.'

Arielle halted and turned to face him. 'I remember a news report that Prince Niels had lost his life in a skiing accident. How can it have been your fault?'

'The skiing trip was my idea. It was meant to be an opportunity for us to spend a few days chilling out together before Niels took on the responsibilities of a husband and the ruler of Fjernland.'

'You didn't make the avalanche happen,' Arielle said gently. She put her hand on his arm. 'Eirik, you can't blame yourself.'

He did not deserve her compassion. 'My mother blames me and rightly so. When we were growing up, my brother was the serious one and I was the clown. I felt it was my role to make sure he had some fun before he devoted the rest of his life to duty. My parents believed I was a bad influence, and so it proved. If I hadn't suggested the skiing holiday Niels would still be here. I will have to live with that for the rest of my life. I am the replacement heir to the throne, and I will choose as my bride a woman who is best suited to be the future Princess Consort.'

Arielle opened the car window and took a deep breath of sea air. Eirik had driven through the busy centre of Fjernland's capital city, Ved Floden. Now they had left the city behind and were on a road that ran parallel to the coast. The sky and sea were forget-me-not blue, but the snow-topped mountains across the bay were a reminder that, despite the spring sunshine, the temperature was in single digits.

She darted a glance at Eirik. Before they had left Princess Catalina's house by the lake, he had changed out of his wet clothes into jeans and a raincloud-grey cashmere sweater, and he looked divine. Conversation between them during the hour and a half journey to the city had been limited to Eirik pointing out places of interest and her mumbling a response.

Arielle shuddered with embarrassment when she remembered how she had practically begged him to make love to her. She did not understand what had come over her. Eirik had revealed a sensual side to her nature that she'd been unaware of, and she had been eager to explore the feelings he aroused in her. To cap it all she had blurted out that her only sexual relationship had been a disaster.

It was not surprising that he had rejected her clumsy advances. And he had made it very clear that she was nothing like the kind of woman he would choose for a wife. But she'd already known that. She did not have a drop of blue blood in her body. Giving a deep sigh, Arielle stared out of the window, glad of the distraction of the stunning scenery.

'The mountains remind me of white meringues,' she murmured. 'Do they always have snow on them?'

'The ice on the summits never melts, unless there is an eruption of course.' Eirik laughed when he glanced at Arielle's startled expression. 'There are several glacier-covered volcanos in Fjernland and two that are currently active. The last time one erupted was twenty years ago.'

His smile made her heart thump madly, and she quickly turned her head to look out of the window again. The buildings next to the coast were mostly single-storey wooden houses. Whereas the city skyline had been dominated by tall office blocks. Eirik had explained that much of Fjernland's wealth came from banking and technology, and tourism was a thriving industry.

'The volcanos are a draw for tourists,' he said now. 'Visitors come hoping to see the aurora borealis, and there are many health spas, which advertise treatments in the natural hot springs. It's a fine balance between the income generated by tourism, and the importance of protecting Fjernland's unique and beautiful landscape.'

Arielle's gaze was drawn to his handsome profile. 'You obviously love your country, but you don't want to rule it.'

'I never said I do not want to be the Sovereign,' he muttered. 'I did not expect that the role would be mine—and I'm not sure I will be any good.' The hint of vulnerability in this strong man tugged on Arielle's heart. 'My brother was taught practically from birth the protocols and duties of being the monarch,' Eirik continued. 'Niels was better suited to royal life than me. He accepted that things have been done the same way for centuries, but I find many of the old ways stuffy and archaic in the twenty-first century.'

'Why don't you change the old ways? I mean, you will be the Reigning Sovereign and you can make the rules. Maybe instead of trying to emulate your brother, you should do things your way.'

He snorted. 'You make it sound simple, but the traditions of the monarchy have stayed the same for hundreds of years.'

'Making changes isn't easy,' Arielle agreed. Her lack of self-confidence stemmed from growing up with her controlling father. Even when she'd become an adult, she had studied for her degree at a university in Cornwall because she'd lacked the courage to move to a different part of the country to escape her father's influence.

Since Gerran Rowse had been sent to prison, she had been a virtual recluse at her studio, fearful of pushing herself out into the wider world where she might be judged by people who had heard of her father's appalling crimes. But thanks to Eirik, she had the chance of working in marine conservation again, and she hoped that her father's notoriety had not reached remote Fjernland. Without Eirik's help, she might never have found the courage to leave Penash.

Arielle surfaced from her thoughts when Eirik

drove through a gateway with a sign above it that read Fjernland Marine Research Institute. He parked the car in front of a large building that was a striking mix of old and new architecture.

'The site used to be owned by Fjernland's biggest brewery,' he explained. 'After a century of beer production here, the company moved to new premises. I saw the potential of the building when I decided to establish the marine research institute. The close proximity to the sea makes it an ideal location, and the laboratories and testing facilities are among the best in the world.'

'Well, I guess this is it,' Arielle said huskily. She pushed a stray curl that had escaped from her chignon, behind her ear, and smoothed an imagined crease from her blue dress.

'There is no need to feel nervous,' Eirik told her. 'Valdemar is impressed with your CV.'

She let him think she was uptight about her interview, but the truth was it had occurred to her that she would probably never meet Eirik again. Soon his father would abdicate and Eirik would become the Reigning Sovereign, and he would be assisted by the woman he chose to be his Princess Consort.

He got out of the car and came round to open her door. His chivalry made her feel like a queen. Arielle forced a bright smile and held out her hand to him. 'Happy birthday in a couple of weeks. And good luck with wife hunting.'

Her heart gave an annoying flutter when Eirik clasped her hand in his strong grasp and lifted her fingers up to his lips to press a light kiss against her knuckles. Arielle knew the gesture was common etiquette in many European countries, including Fjernland apparently, but that did not stop a sizzle of electricity shooting through her. She unconsciously flicked her tongue over her lower lip to moisten it and froze when Eirik's blue eyes blazed.

They were two shooting stars on different trajectories, she reminded herself. But right now, they seemed to be on a collision course as he moved closer to her. She breathed in the sandalwood scent of his cologne and then forgot to breathe at all when he lowered his face towards hers.

'Prince Eirik, it's good to see you.' The voice from behind Arielle shattered the sexual tension. Eirik swore softly and stepped away from her, running a hand through his hair.

'Valdemar, how are you?'

Arielle turned and saw a thick-set man sporting a bushy beard. She felt her colour rise when his curious gaze moved from Eirik to her and back again.

'This is Professor Valdemar Oskarsson,' Eirik told her. 'Valdemar, I'd like you to meet Arielle Tremain.'

'Welcome to Fjernland's Marine Research Institute, Arielle.'

'I'll catch up with you another time,' Eirik said to Valdemar. 'I must leave. My mother is hosting a tea party at the palace, and I promised I would be there.' He nodded to Arielle and shook hands with Valdemar before he strode over to the car.

Moments later he drove away, and a lump formed

in Arielle's throat when the car disappeared from view. She wondered if Ida Lundberg had been invited to tea at the palace. Perhaps Eirik would decide to marry the beautiful blonde and announce their engagement at his birthday ball.

She realised that Valdemar was looking at her curiously. A job at the marine institute was the chance of a lifetime, and it was time she stopped daydreaming about an unobtainable prince and focused on her career, she told herself firmly.

Valdemar ushered her into the building. 'I am very interested in your work exploring new initiatives to recycle plastic waste, which is ruining the world's oceans. Shall we have a chat?'

# CHAPTER SIX

EIRIK GLANCED AROUND the Red Drawing Room at Sejrrig Place where twenty or so guests, mainly young women who had been selected by his mother for their grace, sophistication, and suitability to be his wife, were conversing with each other in well-modulated voices while trying to catch his eye.

He considered drowning himself in the punch bowl. It might liven up the interminably tedious evening, he brooded. But he guessed that the liveried footman whose job was to serve the cocktail, made with fruit, alcohol and spices and known as *glogg* in Fjernland, would rush to pull his head out of the antique, silver-gilt bowl. Besides it would be a waste of good vodka, he decided, taking his fourth—or was it fifth?—glass from the tray.

Drinking himself into a coma was a more inviting option. The buffet supper was the third social event in the past week that his mother had arranged in her self-appointed role of matchmaker. Eirik knew there was no escaping his destiny as Fjernland's Reigning Sovereign, or Princess Hulda's determination that he would marry—tomorrow if she had her way. He had a sense of a tsunami racing towards him that would sweep away his old life and leave him drowning in duty and responsibility.

Where was a mermaid when he needed one?

*Need.* That irritating word again. He assured himself that he did not need Arielle. It was just that he could not stop thinking about her. And until he had got over his fascination, obsession—neither word felt comfortable—with a green-eyed siren, he could not concentrate on the task of choosing a wife.

All evening he had been aware of Princess Hulda's beady eyes on him. And he *had* tried. He'd worked the room, made small talk, and smiled until his face ached. But after two minutes of conversation with the daughter of a French duc, Eirik had known that he was not going to marry Madelaine Blanchet. There was no logical reason why he should not make her his bride. Mademoiselle Blanchet was charming, well educated and her father was a descendant of the brother of Louis XVI, the unfortunate last King of France.

'Madelaine has three brothers,' his mother had informed him before the party, when she had listed the attributes of each female guest. 'It is likely that she would give you a son. I don't know what more you could want.'

Eirik could guess what his mother's reaction would be if he admitted that he wanted a woman with a mermaid's tail and a tangle of russet curls.

Aphrodite with voluptuous curves and eyes the colour of a stormy sea.

'I do wish you would make the effort to be more agreeable.' Princess Hulda's terse voice forced Eirik's mind from the image of Arielle naked in his bed, her riotous hair spread across the pillows.

'How am I not being agreeable?' His tone was curter than he'd intended. He forced a smile in an attempt to lighten the atmosphere between him and his mother, which was frosty at the best of times. 'I have spoken to each of your guests.'

'You have spent the evening pacing around the room like a caged tiger,' Princess Hulda told him waspishly. 'I am devoting all my time and energy in assisting you to find a wife. Is it too much to ask for your cooperation? You practically ignored Ida Lundberg, and the French girl did not hold your attention for long. With your brother gone, it is vital that you have a legitimate heir.'

'Let me reassure you that I am fully aware of what is expected of me,' Eirik gritted. As ever, the reference to Niels evoked a stab of guilt in his gut.

'I am glad to hear it,' his mother said crisply. 'I don't know what has been wrong with you since you returned from England, but you need to deal with it, and quickly.'

'Indeed,' Eirik muttered to himself when Princess Hulda swept away with a rustle of her black taffeta gown. He accepted that it was his duty to marry for the sake of the monarchy. But he realised he must have Arielle first. He had told himself that she was forbidden fruit. But wasn't it always the way that you wanted most what you could not have?

Arielle had said she wanted to make love with him before their lives went in different directions. He would spend a perfect night with her, Eirik decided. He did not doubt that the sex would be incredible. The chemistry between them was white-hot. But in his experience, sexual attraction was transitory, and he was confident that his fascination with Arielle would fade once he had slept with her.

Arielle switched off her laptop and stretched her arms above her head. Her neck and shoulders ached as a result of her sitting at her desk for too long. People often thought that marine conservation work meant spending every day on the beach or diving in the sea, but the truth was that a lot of time was spent in front of a computer. Not that she was complaining. It was wonderful to be doing the job she loved again.

After her interview ten days ago, the head of the marine research institute had offered her a temporary position for six months. Valdemar Oskarsson had said there was a good chance that her role could be made permanent when Prince Eirik became the Reigning Sovereign of Fjernland.

'The Prince donates money to the institute from his personal wealth. When he becomes the Sovereign, he hopes to persuade the principality's National Council to increase funding for marine conservation,' Valdemar had explained. 'Protecting the oceans is something Prince Eirik feels passionate about.'

Arielle had felt herself blush at the memory of Eirik's passion. Fortunately, Valdemar had not seemed to notice her pink cheeks when he had ushered her into one of the laboratories and introduced her to his heavily pregnant wife, Frida. Since then Arielle had been shadowing Frida in preparation for when she took charge of a project to measure microplastic pollution in the North Sea. The work was fascinating and left little time for her to daydream about Eirik.

The other scientists working at the institute were friendly and had invited her for a drink at one of the many lively bars in the area. The nearby coastal town attracted a community of artists, and surfers and divers flocked to the glorious beach. She had moved into an apartment in the same building as the marine institute. Accommodation on the upper floors was for visiting students and researchers, but a flat had been vacant and Valdemar had suggested she could live there while she settled into her new job in a new country. Although small, the apartment was bright and modern, and Arielle loved it.

Her life would be perfect, if only she could forget about Eirik and stop following the daily news coverage about him on social media. It was no secret in Fjernland that His Serene Highness, Prince Otto was prepared to abdicate in favour of his remaining son as soon as Prince Eirik had become betrothed. The media were in a frenzy, trying to guess who his bride and future Princess Consort would be. While his father was recuperating after a recent health scare, Prince Eirik had stood in for Prince Otto at several royal functions and had been accompanied by his mother.

Every photo and news film clip had shown Ida Lundberg in the background. In all probability Eirik would reveal at his birthday ball that he was going to marry the elegant blonde, Arielle thought dismally. And she would be there to witness him make the announcement.

At the beginning of the week Valdemar had handed Arielle an envelope bearing the royal coat of arms. Inside she'd found an invitation to attend the masquerade ball at the Winter Palace.

'Frida and I received our invitations a few weeks ago,' Valdemar explained. 'Representatives from the many organisations, societies and charities that Prince Eirik supports will attend the ball. I spoke to the Prince after I'd offered you a job, and he thought it would be a nice idea to invite the marine institute's newest recruit to the ball. He will send a car for us, and we have been allocated rooms at the palace for the night. The Winter Palace is high up in the mountains, and the journey home would be too much for Frida after the party.'

'I don't own a ball gown,' Arielle had said lamely. It was the only excuse she could think of. She couldn't admit that the idea of going to the ball and seeing Eirik with his future bride would be torture.

'I'm sure you will find something suitable to wear in one of the boutiques in Ved Floden,' Frida had suggested. 'I bought a dress for the ball a few weeks ago. But I've got huge.' She patted her pregnancy bump. 'I'll look like a whale.'

'You will be the most beautiful woman in the ballroom,' Valdemar had assured his wife. The tender look between the couple had caused Arielle a pang of envy. Since her disastrous relationship with Jack, she hadn't dated anyone else. Falling in love seemed a scary prospect. But seeing how happy Valdemar and Frida were had made her realise that loving the right person and being loved in return could be wonderful.

Not that she had any intention of falling in love with Eirik, Arielle told herself sternly. Setting her hopes on an unobtainable prince was a certain route to heartbreak. But at least the problem of a ball gown had been resolved. The previous day, after she'd finished work, the concierge of the apartments had handed her a parcel that had been delivered for her.

She had hurried up to her flat to open the box with the name of a Paris couture house on the front, and gasped when she'd lifted the dress out. It was dark green velvet, with a fitted bodice, low cut at the front and plunging almost to her waist at the back. The skirt clung to her hips before flaring out in a fishtail design to the floor. Arielle had discovered that she could not wear a bra beneath the daring dress. A pair of green velvet, high-heeled shoes and a matching clutch bag completed the outfit, and there was also a beautiful green and gold mask. A note in the box simply bore Eirik's name, and the sight of his bold handwriting had made her heart skip a beat.

The ball was on Thursday evening, and for the

whole day Arielle's emotions lurched between excitement and dread. She had never been inside a royal palace and was never likely to get the opportunity again. As for Eirik, she guessed he had sent her the ball gown as a thank you for saving him after his yacht had sunk. It would be foolish to read anything more into his kind gesture, she told herself. He had probably asked one of his staff to choose a dress for her.

She spent the afternoon in the lab with Frida, analysing samples of microplastics using an infrared imaging machine. Discovering what types of plastics were in the oceans was an important step in the fight to stop the pollution.

'I'll finish typing up the report,' Arielle said when she saw Frida rubbing her back. 'Why don't you put your feet up for a while?'

'I will, if you don't mind. It feels like the baby is playing football inside me.'

'You only have a few more weeks to go, don't you?' Arielle murmured sympathetically.

Frida gave a weary smile. 'To tell you the truth I'm a bit anxious about the birth. Valdemar and I tried to get pregnant for six years before we struck lucky. This baby means everything to us.'

Arielle remembered that Eirik had told her he must marry in order to provide a legitimate heir to the throne. He had stated that love would not be a feature of his marriage, but would he love his child? She hoped so, for she knew what it was like to grow up without loving parents.

Her mother had loved her, but after she had died Arielle had had no one to praise her when she'd done well at school or comfort her when she was unwell. Her father had only noticed her if she'd forgotten to prepare the fire or failed to have his dinner ready when he wanted it. Children needed to feel loved, and so did adults. The loveless marriage that Eirik insisted he wanted sounded like a recipe for disaster.

She smiled at Frida. 'Go home and rest, and I'll see you tonight. The car will be here at six thirty to take us to the palace.'

Hair straighteners were a godsend, Arielle decided later when she studied her reflection in the mirror. Instead of her usual riot of curls, her hair fell in sleek waves to halfway down her back. The dramatic dress required her to wear more make-up than usual. She always used concealer to cover the small scar on her cheek, and for the party she'd emphasised her eyes with a smoky shadow and added a slick of dusky rose gloss to her lips.

The velvet gown moulded her curvy figure, and she hoped it wasn't too obvious that she was braless. The dress managed to be both sexy and sophisticated. It was hard to believe that the woman in the mirror was ordinary Arielle Tremain who had been teased by her classmates for wearing a threadbare school uniform several sizes too small. One of the teachers had taken pity on her and sorted out some second-hand skirts and blouses and a winter coat when she'd explained that her father did not give her money for clothes.

Her old insecurities flooded back. Why had she thought that she could go to a royal ball? She did not belong in Prince Eirik's world. But perhaps experiencing his luxurious lifestyle for one evening would make her accept that she did not stand a chance with him.

Hearing a knock on the door of the apartment, she grabbed her purse and overnight bag and found Valdemar in the corridor. He was wearing jeans rather than a dinner suit as Arielle had expected, and his expression was strained.

'I have to take Frida to the hospital right away. She was feeling unwell, and I asked the midwife to visit. Her blood pressure is too high, and it could be dangerous for her and the baby.' He stared at Arielle's dress. 'Obviously we can't go to the ball.'

'Of course not.' Arielle quashed the selfish stab of disappointment she felt. 'Hospital is the best place for Frida, and I'm sure everything will be all right,' she said gently.

'I hope so.' Valdemar's voice was gruff. 'It is too late to ask any of the other staff from the institute to accompany you to the palace, but you will be a great representative for our work in marine conservation. I sent a message to Prince Eirik explaining that you will be on your own this evening.'

'Oh, I thought…' Butterflies leapt in Arielle's stomach when she realised that Valdemar expected her to attend the ball alone.

He was already striding down the corridor and

called over his shoulder, 'The car to take you to the palace is waiting outside. I must get back to Frida.'

The tall white towers of the Winter Place reached towards an indigo night sky that was scattered with thousands of glittering stars. Beyond the fairy-tale castle loomed craggy mountains with snow-covered peaks. A crescent moon was reflected in the still, black water of the lake in front of the palace.

Arielle wished she had more time to take in the beauty of her surroundings. But the car swept up the gravel driveway, past the line of limousines queuing to deposit party guests at the grand front entrance of the palace. The chauffeur drove on and turned into a small courtyard at the back of the building. He jumped out to open the rear door and when Arielle alighted from the car, she was met by Eirik's private secretary.

'Miss Tremain, please come this way.'

Had she imagined there was disapproval in Gustav's voice? Arielle followed him through a door that she guessed was used by staff and tradesmen and wondered why she had been escorted into the palace secretly, instead of entering through the main door with the other guests. Gustav led her through a maze of corridors before he stopped and ushered her into a room.

Her heart leapt at the idea that Eirik might want to see her in private before the ball got under way. But there was no one in the study. A fire was crackling in the hearth, and the biggest dog she had ever seen stood up and padded over to her.

'He belongs to Prince Eirik,' Gustav told her. 'Maks is devoted to the Prince and takes little interest in anyone else.'

'Hello, boy,' Arielle said softly. She loved all animals and had been heartbroken when Bess, the old border collie that her father had kept as a sheepdog, had died. 'I'm sure you guard your master well.'

The huge dog could have put his paws on her shoulders if he'd wanted to. Arielle held out her hand and patted his smooth golden coat, and after a moment Maks pushed his damp nose into her palm.

'You seem to have won Maks over.' Gustav sounded surprised. He crossed the room and took a flat leather box from the bureau. 'Prince Eirik would like you to have these,' he told Arielle, showing her an exquisite emerald and diamond necklace, and matching earrings.

For a few seconds she was too shocked to speak. Sending her a ball gown was one thing, although she intended to pay Eirik for the dress. But the jewellery must be worth a fortune. She shook her head. 'Please tell the Prince I can't accept such an expensive gift from him.'

'Yes, he anticipated that would be your reaction.' Gustav's voice was marginally warmer. 'However, His Royal Highness insists that you wear the jewellery this evening. You can return the items after the ball if you wish.' He lifted the necklace from the box and held it out to Arielle. 'All the aristocratic young ladies will be wearing tiaras, necklaces and other precious jewels that in many cases are family heirlooms. The Prince hopes that wearing the jewellery will help you to blend in with the other guests,' Gustav said drily.

Feeling that she had to comply, Arielle took the necklace from Gustav. It was heavier than she'd expected, and when she fastened it around her neck, the emeralds and diamonds felt cold against her skin. She removed her faux gold studs, and her hands shook as she attached the emerald drop earrings to her ear lobes. 'I'll be terrified of losing one. Even if I wore the Crown Jewels of England, I still wouldn't be an aristocratic lady,' she said flatly.

'At a masquerade ball you can be whoever you want to be.' Gustav gave something approaching a smile. He helped her to fit her mask over the top part of her face and turned her towards the mirror.

Arielle stared at the reflection of an elegant and exotic woman wearing a couture gown and fabulous jewels and did not recognise herself. None of the other guests at the ball would know that her father was a murderer, or that her integrity had been questioned at his trial, she reassured herself. The judge had believed her testimony that she'd been unaware of Gerran Rowse's crimes. But the Bray family had accused her of lying to try to stop her father from being sent to prison. It wasn't true. Arielle was ashamed of her father and hoped he would rot in jail.

Wearing the masquerade mask gave her anonymity. Gustav was right—tonight she could be someone different from her usual reserved self. At the ball she could be the self-confident woman she wished she were. Her mask would also hide her reaction if Eirik announced his engagement to his future wife. Of course, she *knew* she wasn't princess material, and he would never choose her, but that hadn't stopped her wishing for the moon.

The ballroom was vast and even more opulent than the other rooms Arielle had glimpsed when Gustav had escorted her through the palace. The polished parquet floor gleamed beneath the lights blazing from many chandeliers. Elegant marble columns rose up to meet the frescoed ceiling, and the vibrant blue silk wall panels were edged with gilded mouldings.

She was directed to join the line of female guests standing on one side of the ballroom opposite the men who had formed another line. The young woman next to Arielle looked towards the doorway and said excitedly, 'They'll be here any minute.'

'Who?'

'The royal family. They will make an entrance when all the guests are assembled. Is this your first ball?' Without waiting for Arielle to reply, the woman explained, 'Prince Otto has been ill, and he is not here tonight, so Prince Eirik will escort his mother. As they walk down the room, the women will curtsey to the Prince and the men will bow to Princess Hulda. Then Prince Eirik will choose a partner for the first dance. It's rumoured that he will dance with the woman he intends to marry. Naturally, everyone will try to guess her identity behind her mask. Although his most likely choice of bride is Baron Lundberg's daughter. Ida is easy to spot with her pale blonde hair, and she is wearing a white dress and mask. Perhaps a hint that she will soon be wearing a wedding dress,' the woman said with a heavy sigh.

Arielle's gaze was drawn to the set of doors as they were flung open by footmen and Prince Eirik, with Princess Hulda on his arm, entered the ballroom to a fanfare of trumpets. They walked slowly between the two lines of guests and each woman in turn bobbed a curtsey as Eirik passed by.

He looked breathtaking in a superbly tailored tuxedo that emphasised the broadness of his shoulders. His dark blond hair was swept back from his brow, and a black and gold mask drew attention to his sculpted cheekbones, but of course it could not disguise his identity. He possessed an aura of power and pre-eminence that set him apart from other men.

Arielle's heart thumped as Eirik drew nearer to where she was standing in the line. Her eyes met his intense gaze and she saw something flare in those blue depths that heated her blood. She was conscious of his smouldering scrutiny as he roved his eyes over her velvet gown and sleek hairstyle before lingering on the emeralds and diamonds at her throat. Her breath was trapped in her lungs, and she felt as though only she and Eirik existed.

The strange sense that they belonged to each other body and soul lasted mere seconds before she became aware that Princess Hulda had turned her head and was looking at her. Eirik's mother's coldly assessing stare sent a shiver through Arielle, and she released a shaky breath when the Prince and Princess walked on.

When they reached the far end of the room, Eirik led his mother to a chair and waited for her to be seated. There was a tangible air of expectation in the ballroom as he strode over to the line of women.

'Oh! That's a surprise. Prince Eirik has chosen Princess Matilda for the first dance,' the woman beside Arielle murmured.

'Does that mean she is the woman he intends to marry?' Arielle craned her neck to see Eirik's dance partner. There were so many beautiful young women at the ball, and she supposed that Princess Matilda was one of them.

'I shouldn't think so. Princess Matilda is Prince Eirik's elderly aunt and Prince Otto's sister. It seems that the Prince intends to keep everyone guessing who his bride will be for a while longer.'

Eirik and his aunt began a slow waltz. The male guests stepped forward to claim the women opposite them for the dance. Gustav offered Arielle his hand. 'May I have the pleasure of this dance, Miss Tremain? Prince Eirik asked me to look after you at the ball,' he said when she looked uncertain.

'I've never done ballroom dancing before,' Arielle admitted as the private secretary led her around the dance floor, and she accidentally trod on his foot.

'My bruised toes are testament to that fact,' Gustav replied in his dry voice. 'I will attempt to teach you the rudiments of a simple box step. When I take a step forward with my right foot, you step backwards with your left, then we both step to the side and finally bring the feet together to the count of three.'

She got the hang of it after a while. A brief interlude in the music played by the orchestra was a cue for the dancers to change partners for the next dance. As Arielle moved around the ballroom with a number of different dance partners she was determined not to look for Eirik, but his height and sheer physical presence drew her gaze to him.

Her heart sank when she saw him dancing with a tall, willowy woman with pale blonde hair piled on top of her head in an elaborate chignon. The woman was wearing an exquisite white ball gown and a mask decorated with white feathers. Ida Lundberg was as elegant as a swan, and her regal bearing would make her a perfect wife and Princess Consort for Prince Eirik. That seemed to be the opinion of the other guests when Arielle had overheard snippets of their conversations.

At that moment Eirik looked across the ballroom directly at her. He must have seen her as clearly as she saw him, but he gave no sign of recognition and turned his head away. His dismissal made it clear that he had no personal interest in her and had invited her to the ball simply because she was a representative of the marine research institute that he supported.

'Would you like some champagne?' asked the young man Arielle was dancing with.

She smiled at him and ignored the thought that she

would like to escape to her room in the guest wing of the palace, crawl under the duvet and have a good cry. 'I'd love some.' Tonight was her one and only chance to attend a royal ball, and she was going to enjoy every minute of it, Arielle told herself sternly. Life was about embracing new experiences, not moping over a prince who she had known from the outset could never be hers.

The champagne helped, and after a couple of glasses of fizz, and finding there was no shortage of men who wanted to dance with her, she discovered that she was genuinely having a good time. She even had the confidence to flirt a little with her dance partners, and a few times when there was a lull in the music the sound of her laughter turned heads in her direction.

'You seem to be having fun.' Eirik's deep voice was close to her ear. Arielle's stomach muscles clenched when she turned her head and found him beside her. With effortless grace and a gleam of determination in his eyes, he drew her away from the man she had been dancing with. Spinning her round to face him, he captured her hand in his and placed his other hand on her waist.

'Isn't having fun the point of a party?' she asked breathlessly as she rested her free hand on his shoulder and tried to remember what to do with her feet.

'You call this evening fun?' Eirik demanded tersely. 'Every move I make is watched by three hundred and fifty guests, and my mother is in one of her sulks because I refuse to allow her to interfere in my life.'

'I suppose your mother is annoyed because you haven't made an announcement of your betrothal.' Arielle tensed when Eirik's thigh brushed against hers. Even through his trousers and her velvet dress she was aware of the ripple of his hard muscles. The contact felt shockingly intimate. 'Ida Lundberg must be disappointed. Everyone expects that you will choose her to be your bride after she was seen with you at royal events in the past two weeks.'

'I attended a number of functions with Princess Hulda, and Ida was there because my mother recently appointed her as a lady-in-waiting.'

'Are you sure that was the only reason?' Arielle muttered. 'I saw you dancing with Ida this evening and the two of you looked perfect together.'

'Ida was not the only woman I danced with. Were you jealous, my green-eyed mermaid?'

She looked away from his speculative gaze. 'I had no right to feel jealous,' she said stiffly.

'I had no right to wish I could tear you away from every man I watched you dance with,' Eirik growled. 'As for the men who have undressed you with their eyes, I would take great delight in rearranging their features with my fist.'

She flushed. 'No one has undressed me with their eyes…have they?'

'Do you have any idea how beautiful you are? Or how incredibly sexy you look in that dress? I chose it from the designer's website because I knew it would be perfect for you. But you exceeded all my expectations. When I walked into the ballroom you blew my mind.'

Eirik's huskily spoken words sent a quiver of response through Arielle. She stumbled and he tightened his hand on her waist. He winced when her stiletto heel came down on his foot.

'Sorry. One back, two to the side, three together,' she said under her breath.'

His brows lifted. 'What are you doing?'

'Gustav showed me how to waltz. But I forget the steps if I am distracted.'

He laughed softly. 'Do I distract you, *skatta*?'

The sensual musk of his aftershave was all around her. The ballroom was full of people, but Arielle only saw him. She nodded, and his eyes glittered as he slid his arm around her waist and placed his hand on her bare back where her dress was cut away. His touch burned her, and she did not try to resist when he drew her closer so that they were hip to hip. 'Dancing is easy,' he murmured. 'Let me show you.'

The orchestra had struck up a fairly quick waltz and Arielle's feet flew over the floor as Eirik whisked her around the ballroom. She had wanted to be in his arms all evening, and she stopped telling herself the reasons why this was a bad idea and melted against his hard body.

'You're a good dancer,' she said breathlessly.

'My mother insisted that my brother and I took ballroom-dancing lessons every Saturday morning when we were younger. I would much rather have gone sailing, so I learned the steps quickly.'

'I suppose you attend a lot of parties and being able to dance must be a useful skill to have.'

His sexy smile stole Arielle's breath. 'I have many skills,' he whispered into her ear. The stubble on his jaw scraped over her cheek, and she knew that if she turned her head a fraction their mouths would meet. She would not have believed it was possible to make love on a crowded dance floor, but when Eirik slid his hand down to her bottom and hauled her even closer to him, so that her breasts were pressed against his chest and she felt the hard ridge of his arousal nudge her thigh, Arielle realised that he was seducing her, and she did not want him to stop.

# CHAPTER SEVEN

ARIELLE COULD HAVE danced with Eirik all night, but, as the strains of the 'Blue Danube' faded away, the spell he had cast on her shattered when she saw Princess Hulda standing at the edge of the dance floor, watching them. The Princess beckoned imperiously to her son. Eirik gave a deep sigh and lowered his arms down to his sides.

'My mother wishes to meet you.' His unemotional voice gave no clue to his thoughts. He rested his hand lightly on the base of Arielle's spine and ushered her across the ballroom.

'Mama, I would like to introduce Miss Arielle Tremain from Cornwall in England.'

Arielle remembered that she was supposed to curtsey. She managed an inelegant bob but was hampered by her figure-hugging dress. 'Your Highness,' she mumbled.

Princess Hulda was wearing a black satin ball gown with a voluminous skirt made up of layers of ruffles, which had the unfortunate effect of emphasising her rather dumpy figure. Her silver hair was swept off her face in a severe style, and around her throat was a necklace of blood-red rubies.

The Princess gave Arielle an assessing look. 'Do your family own land in Cornwall, Miss Tremain?'

'Er…no, ma'am. We had a smallholding and kept a few sheep, but the land and cottage were rented.'

'Is your father successful in business?'

Arielle froze. 'My father?' She pictured Gerran Rowse the last time she had seen him as he had been led away from the court to begin a life sentence in prison. He had not looked at her once during the trial, but he'd never been interested in his daughter.

'Arielle does not have any family,' Eirik said, breaking the awkward silence that had fallen while she'd tried to think of something to say.

'How sad.' Princess Hulda's eyes were light grey, almost colourless, and cold. 'That is a very beautiful necklace you are wearing. A family heirloom, perhaps?'

'Um…no.' Arielle could not explain to herself why she was reluctant to tell the Princess that Eirik had lent her the emeralds to wear to the ball. She was relieved when Princess Hulda turned her gaze on her son. The dismissal was subtle, but Arielle felt as unimportant as the Princess had obviously intended her to feel.

'Eirik, I am feeling a little weary. I would like you to escort me to my private sitting room and ask my lady-in-waiting to come to me. I believe you will find Ida with Baron Lundberg in the orangery.'

'Of course, Mama.' Eirik's expression was unreadable. He turned to Arielle and said coolly, 'I hope you enjoy the rest of the ball, Miss Tremain.'

Princess Hulda took her son's arm and did not glance at Arielle. She might as well have been invisible, she thought as she watched Eirik escort his mother out of the ballroom. There were several hundred guests at the ball, but Arielle had never felt more alone. She touched the emerald necklace that Eirik had arranged for her to wear so that she fitted in with the high-society guests. Why had she thought she could belong in his rarefied world for even a few hours?

No one took any notice of her when she walked out of the ballroom. She looked for Gustav, hoping to return the necklace and earrings to him, but there was no sign of him, and she soon lost her way when she tried to find the study, thinking she could replace the jewellery in the bureau.

A damp nose nudged her hand. Eirik's dog, Maks, trotted down the corridor and Arielle followed him. 'You want to go outside, do you?' she said as the dog scratched on a door. Through the window she could see a dark garden. An icy blast of air struck her when she opened the door. Maks nudged her again as if he wanted her to follow him. 'Can you just get on and do what you need to do?' she told him. 'It's freezing out here.'

The frost on the lawn sparkled in the starlight. Arielle hugged her arms around her as the big dog gently pushed her along the path. In the pearly glimmer of the moon, she saw a wooden arbour and Eirik sprawled on the bench seat. Her heart hammered as she walked towards him and felt his intense blue gaze on her.

He had removed his masquerade mask, and the moonlight danced over his sculpted cheekbones. His bow tie was hanging open and he'd unfastened the top buttons of his shirt. Arielle recalled photos in celebrity magazines of a dissolute, playboy prince who had often been snapped by the paparazzi on a superyacht in St Tropez or at a nightclub in some European hotspot or other, invariably with a supermodel on his arm. But she had glimpsed another side to Eirik. He was not just a handsome hunk with a surfeit of charisma. He was trying to come to terms with his brother's death and the role that had been thrust on him as the future monarch.

He stood up and patted the dog's head. 'Well done, Maks. You can go now.'

Arielle watched the dog trot back up the path towards the palace. 'How did he know to bring me here?'

'I told him to.' Noticing her look of surprise, Eirik murmured, 'Animals understand more than humans think they do. But Maks is exceptional. I've had him since he was a few days old. He was the runt of a litter. The gamekeeper wanted pups who would grow into strong hunting dogs, and he was going to let Maks die. But I thought he deserved a chance, so I kept him. I had to feed him from a bottle at first. The funny thing is that Maks grew up to be bigger and stronger than his siblings.'

She could very easily lose her heart to this man, Arielle thought ruefully.

Eirik frowned when he noticed her shiver. 'You are cold. Here, wear this.' He slipped his jacket off and draped it around her shoulders. The silk lining carried the heat of his body and the heady scent of his cologne.

'I shouldn't be here…with you,' she said huskily.

He lifted his hand and wound a lock of her hair around his finger. 'I like your hair like this, but I miss your curls.'

She gave a breathless laugh. 'Oh, they'll bounce back. You should see my crazy hair first thing in the morning.'

'I would like to.' His voice was deeper than Arielle had ever heard it, and, despite the warmth of his jacket, she shivered again. 'I have imagined you naked in my bed, *skatta.* Your red curls spread across my pillows.'

'You shouldn't say things like that.' She clung to her sanity as if it were a life raft and she were adrift in a stormy sea.

'It's the truth.' He moved closer, and Arielle's eyes were drawn to where his shirt was open at his throat. She longed to undo the rest of the buttons and run her hands over his bare chest. 'For the past two weeks I have tried to forget you,' he growled, not disguising his frustration. 'But tonight at the ball it was hopeless. The only woman I saw was you.'

Eirik moved his other hand behind her head and untied the ribbons that secured her mask. It slipped to the ground, but neither of them noticed. His warm breath formed a gossamer cloud in the cold air, and Arielle's lips parted of their own volition in anticipation of his kiss.

'You are the only woman I want,' he said in a low voice that sent another tremor through her.

Whatever was happening, whatever was about to happen, would only be for tonight. She accepted that she could never be part of Eirik's world. But she desired him with every fibre of her body. Need made her breasts ache and evoked a deeper, more insistent throb low in her pelvis. Arielle knew she would regret it for ever if she turned down this chance to make love with the most fascinating man she'd ever met.

Eirik's arms came round her—at last. He pulled her against his whipcord body, and he felt so good, so male and strong. Safe. Arielle tilted her face up to his in mute surrender and watched his eyes blaze.

'Let me warm you,' he whispered against her lips.

'Yes.' Her answer was lost as he covered her mouth with his and kissed her beneath the stars.

Eirik lifted Arielle into his arms and carried her through the frosty garden. She rested her head on his shoulder and he breathed in her seductive perfume. Soon she would be his. The thought caused his pulse to accelerate, and he quickened his steps.

He had left a side door unlocked and there were no guards on duty, meaning that he could enter the palace unseen. This was not how he'd anticipated the evening would end, although in truth he had fantasised about making love to Arielle. He felt a stab of guilt as he acknowledged his failure to do what was expected of him by the Crown Prince and Princess, and by the entire population of Fjernland, it seemed. He was no closer to deciding who to marry, but he'd been aware that there would be fevered speculation at the ball about who might be his future bride.

Unfortunately, he'd taken one look at a green-eyed siren, as sexy as hell in a gown that showed off her gorgeous curves, and his blood had rushed to his groin. He had been certain that he could control his lust for Arielle, but he'd failed spectacularly, and he did not care.

No doubt tomorrow, in the cold light of day, he would question what it was about this woman that made him desperate to strip her naked and explore every inch of her creamy skin with his hands and mouth until she begged for his possession. Not that she would have to beg very hard, Eirik thought self-derisively. The truth was that he needed to be inside Arielle as quickly as possible.

He took the back staircase and corridors up to his private suite of rooms. There was no risk of being spotted by the staff, who would all be downstairs to begin clearing up after the ball had finished and assisting the guests to their cars.

'I can walk,' Arielle protested. 'I'm too heavy for you to carry me up the stairs.'

'Nonsense.' His heart was thundering, but not from physical exertion. He could have carried Arielle to the top of the highest mountain in Fjernland. Desire pulsed in his blood and in his sex. He was descended from Vikings, and he was impatient to claim his shield maiden. Shouldering the door to his apartment, he carried her through to the bedroom and set her down on her feet next to the bed.

'Wow, this is amazing.' Arielle's eyes widened when she looked around the room that was as ornate as the rest of the Winter Palace. The four-poster bed with its gold brocade drapes was not to Eirik's taste, but he had inherited the palace and soon he would inherit the crown and, somehow, he would have to make his peace with the life that awaited him.

But tonight he would not think about the future. The huge bed was a perfect playground for what he had in mind, and he felt his body tauten as he pictured Arielle sprawled on the satin sheets.

'I did not bring you here to admire the decor,' he muttered against her mouth before he kissed her again and again. Her eager response as she parted her lips and kissed him back stoked the fire in his belly. 'I want to see you naked.'

He eased away from her a fraction and stared at the soft flush on her lovely face and those sea green eyes, which right now were glazed with desire. The sirens of ancient legends had sung an intoxicating song that lured men to their doom. Arielle's soft moans of delight as he cradled her breasts in his hands might well be the end of him, Eirik thought. But he did not care, and that in itself should trouble him. With other women he had always remained in control of his sexual urges, but his hunger for Arielle was a voracious beast that demanded to be appeased.

He stood behind her and pushed her glossy hair over her shoulder to expose the slender column of her neck. She tasted of honey and roses when he pressed his lips to her spine and kissed his way down her bare back. His fingers deftly unzipped her dress before he turned her to face him and slid the velvet gown from her shoulders.

Eirik had spent an unseemly amount of time during the ball wondering if Arielle could have worn some sort of bra beneath the backless dress. Now he had his answer and his body clenched.

Her breasts were perfect, round handfuls, tipped with dusky pink nipples that swelled against his tongue when he closed his lips around one taut peak and then the other. The sound of her swiftly indrawn breath delighted him, for it told him that Arielle was as much at the mercy of this inconvenient desire as he was.

With increasing urgency, he tugged the clingy velvet over her hips, and the dress fell to the floor, leaving her in a pair of tiny knickers and gossamer-fine stockings with bands of lace around her thighs.

'Have you any idea what you do to me?' he growled, enjoying her reaction when he traced the top of one stocking before moving his fingers higher to caress the creamy skin of her inner thigh.

'Eirik?' She whispered his name and he laughed softly at her husky plea.

'Tell me what you want, *skatta*.'

'I can't.' She blushed and seemed suddenly vulnerable, dropping her gaze from his. 'I told you that I'm not very good at this.'

He remembered the ex-boyfriend who Arielle had said hadn't satisfied her. She had told him she wasn't a virgin, but Eirik suspected she was not very experienced.

He slid his hand beneath her chin and tilted her face up, forcing her to meet his gaze. 'I am very good at sex,' he murmured. It was not a boast—he had a high sex drive and enjoyed giving his lovers pleasure as much as he enjoyed receiving it. The idea that her ex had not taken the time to ensure that sex was good for Arielle, and from the sound of it had made her feel that it was her failure, made Eirik determined to show her how pleasurable love-making could be. They had all night, and he intended to satiate his damnable desire for her by the morning.

'Why don't we begin with me touching you, and you tell me if you like what I am doing, or if you want me to stop? Does that sound okay?'

She nodded but still looked uncertain. He could not resist kissing the tense line of her mouth until her lips softened beneath his. At the same time, he cradled her breast in his palm and rubbed his thumb across her nipple, eliciting a husky moan from Arielle.

'Do you like it when I do that?'

'Y-yes.'

'What about when I do this?' His other hand was still resting on her stocking top. He felt her thigh quiver when he skimmed his fingers over her sensitive flesh, higher and higher until he pressed his thumb against the moist panel of her panties.

'Yes,' she said in a breathy whisper that made Eirik even harder. 'I…like that.'

'And now?' He slipped his fingers beneath her knickers and his heart gave a kick when he discovered that she was wet down there. Wet for him. The sweet scent of her feminine arousal inflamed his desire. He gently parted her and pushed a finger between her silken folds. 'Do you like what I am doing to you now, *skatta*?'

'Yes. Oh, don't stop.' She pressed herself closer to him, inviting him to continue caressing her. The frantic jerk of her pelvis against his hand melted his frozen heart a little when it occurred to him that perhaps she had never been pleasured in this way before. *Faen.* She was so innocent, and he wanted to teach her everything.

'I have no intention of stopping,' Eirik promised. 'But we will be more comfortable on the bed.' He lifted her onto the mattress, removed her shoes and panties and rolled her sheer stockings down her legs. 'This is how I pictured you when I chose the jewellery for you to wear to the ball,' he said hoarsely. 'Naked in my bed and adorned with emeralds that match the colour of your eyes.'

The feral gleam in Eirik's eyes shocked and excited Arielle. No man had ever looked at her as he was doing, as if he wanted to devour her. Desire sharpened his features so that his skin seemed to be stretched tightly over his high cheekbones. He stared at her mouth as she flicked her tongue across her lower lip.

'I want to make love to you.' His voice was harsh with need and sent a thrill through her.

It hardly seemed possible that she—ordinary Arielle Tremain, who had changed her name to hide the dark secret in her past—could be responsible for Eirik's transformation from an urbane prince to a hungry wolf.

He knelt on the bed and straddled her with his knees on either side of her hips and his hands beside her head. 'You want me too, don't you, my beautiful siren?'

Oh, she did, with a desperation that stunned her. She had never felt this turned on with her ex. She'd only slept with Jack because he had expected her to. Her lack of confidence had made her believe that a dud boyfriend was better than no boyfriend. But Eirik was nothing like Jack, and her instincts told her that sex with him was not going to be a disappointing fumble under the duvet.

'How can I please you?' Eirik asked softly.

Arielle bit her lip, reluctant to admit her experience of sex was so limited that she did not know what she would enjoy. 'It seems unfair that I'm naked and you are still dressed,' she murmured.

He sat back on his heels and gave her a sexy grin. Taking her hands, he placed them on his shirt front. 'Feel free to undress me, *musaling*.'

Arielle had never undressed anyone other than herself. With unsteady fingers she undid a button on his shirt. 'What is *musaling*?'

'It means little mouse.'

She frowned. 'Mice are drab and unexciting.' Was that how Eirik saw her?

'I disagree. They are cute, timid creatures.'

'Nothing like me, then.' Was there a more unflattering description than *timid*? Determined to show him that she wasn't a nervous almost-novice—even though she was—she tore open the rest of the buttons and pushed the shirt off his shoulders.

His body was hot in every sense. She ran her hands over his golden skin and felt the soft abrasion of his chest hairs against her palms. The ridges of his abdominal muscles fascinated her as she skimmed her fingertips over the fuzz of blond hairs that arrowed down to the waistband of his trousers.

It was stupid to feel shy, Arielle told herself as she hesitated before undoing his belt. Her breath caught in her throat when she put her hand on his trouser zip and discovered the unmistakable proof of his arousal. He groaned as she tugged the zip down and her nails scraped over the bulge of his manhood.

'I'll take it from here,' Eirik growled. He levered himself off the bed and quickly stripped off the rest of his clothes. His eyes locked with Arielle's wide gaze as he pulled his boxers over his hips to reveal his impressive erection. Her heart missed a beat as she tried to imagine him sliding his swollen length inside her.

Naked, he was a work of art: long-limbed and lean-hipped, a washboard-flat stomach and that broad, muscular chest. A Viking prince with searing passion in his eyes. The air was thick with sexual tension. Arielle's breathing was shallow, and her heart was racing as Eirik stepped closer to the bed and put his hands on her thighs, gently pushing them apart. He dropped onto his knees, and she trembled when she realised his intention. Her secret sexual fantasy was for a lover to put his mouth on her, and she could hardly believe that it was going to happen.

With slow, deliberate movements that heightened her anticipation, he hooked her legs over his shoulders and slid his hands beneath her bottom to lift her towards him. And then he buried his head between her thighs and flicked his tongue lightly over her opening.

Arielle's whole body jolted in reaction. What Eirik was doing was shockingly intimate, especially as, really, she hardly knew him. But it did not matter. Nothing mattered except that he should continue his wicked caresses with his tongue. She felt utterly wanton with her legs spread wide open while he pleasured her, and it was better than she could ever have imagined.

He quickly took her to the brink, and she curled her fingers into the sheet, dimly aware that the husky moans that filled the room came from her. Eirik's hands were busy too, and the sensation of him sliding a finger inside her and gently stretching her, while simultaneously he closed his mouth over the sensitive nub of her clitoris, sent her over the edge. Her orgasm swept through her in rippling waves of pleasure.

When Arielle came back to earth, tears pricked her eyes. Eirik's consideration and patience as he'd brought her to a climax threatened to dismantle the barriers that she knew she must keep around her heart.

He stood up and rolled a condom over his thick length before he joined her on the bed. But even then, he did not rush her. Only his ragged voice as he muttered, 'You drive me insane, *skatta*,' reassured her that his need was as great as hers.

Propped up on one elbow, he was a golden god with his dark blond hair falling across his brow. He idly trailed his hand over her body, discovering the fragile line of her collarbone before moving down to cup her breast. He bent his head and took her tight nipple into his mouth. The sensation of him sucking hard sent a sharp tug of desire down to Arielle's feminine core. He transferred his mouth to her other breast, and she gasped when he slipped his hand between her legs.

'You are ready for me,' he said softly as he explored her slick heat with his fingers once more. 'I can't wait much longer.'

Nor could she. 'I don't want to wait. I want you,' she whispered. She moved her hand between their bodies and stroked her fingers along the length of his erection, eliciting a groan from him.

'Not this time,' he said, pushing her hand away. 'I'm about to explode.' He positioned himself over her, and the hard gleam in his eyes made Arielle's tummy flip. 'Open your legs wider.'

She complied with his hoarse command and held her breath when he lowered his big body so that the tip of his shaft pressed against her opening. Slowly he eased forwards and entered her, filling her inch by incredible inch. She shifted her hips as the sensation of fullness intensified.

'Am I hurting you?'

'No.' She stared into his blue eyes, touched by his concern. But it was unnecessary. She was on fire for him, and more than anything she wanted him to reach the heights of sexual fulfilment that he had taken her to moments ago. When he withdrew a little way, she tilted her pelvis and slid her hands around his back, gripping his buttocks and urging him to thrust deeper inside her.

Eirik muttered something in Fjernlandic and rested his brow against hers. 'This is *so* good for me, but I need it to be good for you too.'

'It is, or it will be if you stop talking.'

His low rumble of laughter curled around her heart, and she felt a connection between them that was more than physical.

'No more talking,' he promised. He began to move, setting a devastating rhythm that Arielle found utterly addictive. She wrapped her legs around his hips as he drove into her faster, deeper. The orgasm he had given her with his mouth had been amazing, but now her body craved more. She sensed there was something even more intense, but it remained frustratingly beyond her reach.

'Relax, and it will happen,' Eirik murmured. He slipped his hand between their joined bodies and did something wickedly inventive with his fingers. At the same time he gave a hard thrust that drove the breath from her lungs and the world exploded. Her orgasm was so powerful, so pleasurable that Arielle lost all sense of time and place. Sensation after sensation tore through her as her vaginal muscles clenched and unclenched in the sweetest release.

Eirik was still plunging into her, faster, faster. She sensed his urgency and arched her hips to meet every vigorous thrust. He tensed and stared down at her. His eyes glittered, and his breath came in harsh pants, and then his face twisted, and he let out a savage groan as he gave one final, hard thrust. His big body shuddered with the force of his climax before he collapsed on top of her.

Arielle welcomed the weight of him pressing her into the mattress. She locked her arms around his back and turned her face into his neck. When she kissed his skin, she tasted the salt of his sweat. She wished they could stay there for ever, their limbs entwined and hearts thundering in unison. But wishes rarely came true, and after a while Eirik lifted himself off her and moved across the bed.

She missed the illusion of security when she had been in his arms and fought the temptation to snuggle up to him. 'That shouldn't have happened,' she said, getting in first before he told her that he regretted what they had done.

'Probably not,' he agreed. There was amusement in his voice. He rolled onto his side and leaned up on one elbow, stroking damp tendrils of hair off Arielle's face. She told herself that she must have imagined tenderness in his eyes. 'But it did happen,' he murmured. 'And very soon it will happen again.'

He grinned at her startled expression and caught hold of her hand, holding it against his burgeoning arousal. 'We have all night to enjoy each other, and I don't intend to waste a second, *min prinsessa.*'

# CHAPTER EIGHT

EIRIK WOKE TO the soft greyness before dawn. He opened his eyes and watched a finger of faint light poke through the chink in the curtains. A new day heralded a return to reality.

Last night with Arielle had been incredible. His muscles ached from the excesses of the most amazing sex he'd ever had. He'd made love to her several times and when finally their mutual desire had been sated, she had curled up against him like a sleepy kitten. He had slept deeply for the first time since his brother's death, but now thinking of Niels opened the lid of Pandora's box and reminded him that he must put duty before his personal desires.

It was a pity he had not remembered his duty last night, Eirik thought grimly. He turned his head on the pillow and studied a still sleeping Arielle. The sleek hairstyle she'd worn at the ball had reverted to its natural tumble of silky curls, and her auburn eyelashes made crescents on her cheeks. The sheet had slipped down to reveal one creamy breast tipped with a dusky pink nipple that Eirik knew would harden against his tongue if he succumbed to the temptation to put his mouth on her.

The night had exceeded all his expectations, but today he had a full diary of royal duties to perform. He frowned as he remembered how in the throes of passion he had called Arielle his princess. Of course she never could be the Princess Consort. Even if the rules on who he could marry were changed, he would not choose Arielle to be his wife. Not because he cared about their perceived difference in social status. He firmly believed that all people were equal, and it was down to fate that he had been born a prince. But a tragic twist of fate had made him the future monarch. It was his fault that the only person he had ever truly loved was dead, and Eirik assured himself that he did not want or deserve love. The woman he married would have to understand that he expected the relationship to be uncluttered by emotions.

He acknowledged that he did not know Arielle very well, but he suspected she was highly emotional, romantic, and looking for love. He needed to make it clear that she would not find it with him. The way to do that was not to pull the sheet away from her body and settle himself between her thighs to arouse her with his tongue. Remembering how much she had enjoyed him caressing her in that way, and the husky moans she'd made when she'd climaxed against his mouth, made him instantly hard.

Swearing beneath his breath, Eirik slid out of bed and headed for the en suite bathroom to take a cold shower. Standing beneath the punishing spray, he tried to fathom why he was finding it hard to walk away from Arielle when he'd never had a problem compartmentalising his previous lovers in a file marked temporary. Possibly it was because Arielle had seen him at his most vulnerable when she'd saved him from the sea, he brooded. He felt a connection with her. He liked her and he was interested in her marine conservation work. Perhaps they could have been friends if he hadn't let his libido overrule his common sense.

Who was he kidding? he mocked himself when he went into his dressing room and donned the uniform he was required to wear to a military ceremony he was to attend later. He did not want a platonic friendship with Arielle. He had hoped that sleeping with her would release him from her siren's spell. Surely, novelty had been part of her attraction. The thrill of the chase and her ultimate surrender.

But when he returned to the bedroom and saw Arielle still sprawled on the satin sheets, her red curls spilling over the pillow, Eirik was sorely tempted to wake Sleeping Beauty with a kiss that would quickly escalate into tumultuous passion, and he knew that he was in trouble.

'Arielle, wake up.' Eirik's curt voice pulled Arielle from an erotic dream in which she'd relived the many and varied ways he had made love to her throughout the night. But he did not sound like the sexy lover who had groaned her name when she'd wriggled down the bed and flicked her tongue along the length of his manhood.

Reluctantly, she opened her eyes and stared at a stranger. Eirik was resplendent in a dark blue suit decorated with gold buttons and epaulettes. A red silk sash was draped across one shoulder and tied around his waist. Attached to his jacket were several military medals. With his blond hair swept back from his brow and the stubble on his jaw neatly trimmed, he looked like the handsome Prince Charming beloved of fairy tales. But he was remote and unsmiling. Clearly he hadn't read the part of the story where he was meant to wake her with a kiss.

'You need to get up,' he told her.

'I gather that my presence in your bedchamber is no longer required, Your Highness,' she said drily, determined not to let him see that she was hurt by his brusqueness. She sat up and snatched the sheet over her breasts.

A dull flush ran along his cheekbones. 'We both knew that we could only spend one night together.'

She nodded. It was true, but she hadn't expected him to dismiss her quite so brutally. 'Give me five minutes and I'll be out of your hair.' Her voice was as cool as his. She saw a pool of green velvet on the floor where her ball gown had landed when Eirik had undressed her the previous night. 'I left my overnight bag with a change of clothes in my room in the guest wing of the palace.'

'I had Gustav bring your things here to my private suite.' Eirik indicated her bag on a chair. 'I'll leave you to get dressed. I have an appointment this morning and Gustav will drive you back to the marine institute.'

But he continued to stand at the foot of the bed and his eyes narrowed when Arielle inched across the mattress and stood up, clutching the sheet around her to hide her nakedness. 'It's a bit late for modesty,' he drawled. 'Last night I kissed every inch of your body.'

'Last night we were lovers, but now we are not.' Tears threatened, and she wished he would go, before she suffered the humiliation of breaking down in front of him. 'I assume from your uniform and the impressive row of medals on your chest that you are going to a royal event.'

'A passing out parade at the naval college. It's an important day for the cadets and I will preside over the ceremony as the High Commander of Fjernland's Navy.'

'I didn't know that Fjernland had its own military.'

'We work in conjunction with the Danish armed forces. As a matter of fact, I earned the medals I'm wearing when I served as a naval officer for four years. For some of that time I was based on a patrol ship in the Arctic, and my unit was involved with monitoring pollutants including plastic waste on Arctic ecosystems. It was what led me to establish the Fjernland Marine Research Institute, to try to protect the oceans.'

'When you become the Reigning Sovereign you will be able to focus on issues that you believe are important and introduce changes if you deem them necessary for the good of the country.' Arielle wondered if Eirik was aware that there was pride in his voice whenever he mentioned Fjernland. He cared about the principality and the people he would rule. 'Maybe being the monarch won't be as bad as you think.'

He stared at her. 'Maybe not,' he said gruffly. 'Arielle...'

'We are two stars on different trajectories.' She remembered what he had said at the cottage in Penash, a lifetime ago it seemed. 'For what it's worth I think you will be a great Sovereign.'

He took a step towards her and swore when there was a knock on the outer door of the suite. Pulling back the sleeve of his jacket to check his watch, he said in a frustrated voice, 'I have to leave, or I will be late for the ceremony.' Eirik strode over to the door and halted. He turned around and even across the distance of the bedroom Arielle felt the heat of his gaze. 'I am not ready for this, us, to end,' he growled.

He was killing her. Arielle's heart missed a beat at *us*. But she reminded herself that all Eirik wanted was sex, while she was in imminent danger of falling in love with him. 'It must end,' she said quietly. 'You know it must. I can never be part of your world.'

'Good morning, Miss Tremain.' Gustav stood up when Arielle walked into the sitting room. He studied her skinny jeans and oversized jumper that had a habit of slipping off her shoulder and Arielle wondered if he was comparing her to elegant Ida Lundberg. She felt his sharp gaze on her pink-rimmed eyes and told herself she did not care what Eirik's private secretary thought of her.

'I'm ready to leave,' she said stiffly.

Gustav escorted her along numerous corridors that Arielle guessed were for the staff's use, and they left the palace unnoticed via a back door. Clearly Eirik did not want anyone other than his most trusted servant to know that he had spent the night with a commoner, she thought dismally.

Eirik's dog bounded up and pushed his nose into her hand. 'Goodbye, Maks,' she said in a choked voice, stroking his golden head. Gustav had put her bag in the boot of the car, and now he was talking on his phone. He spoke in Fjernlandic and glanced at Arielle a couple of times. She climbed onto the back seat and shook her head at Maks when he leapt into the car. 'I'd love to take you with me, but I'm afraid I can't.'

'Maks can come along for the ride,' Gustav said as he slid behind the wheel.

The big dog rested his head on Arielle's knee, and she was glad of his company. She closed her eyes as the smooth motion of the car had a soporific effect on her after her energetic night, memories of which brought a flush to her cheeks. Maybe she would get a dog when she settled somewhere, she mused. She had decided not to extend her contract at the Fjernland Marine Research Institute after her six months was up. Eirik would no doubt have married by then and seeing news coverage of him with his wife would be painful. But she had more confidence to look for another marine conservation job now. Valdemar was impressed with her work and would give her a good reference.

Arielle wondered if Frida had had the baby. The last message she'd received from Valdemar had said that it might be necessary to induce the birth earlier than Frida's due date. Hopefully she would find out more when she returned to the marine institute, Arielle thought. But when she looked out of the car window, she was surprised to see that the road was climbing higher, and the snow-capped mountains seemed closer.

Gustav drove along a track that ran beside a turquoise lake. The skyline was dominated by a towering mountain. The snow on the summit sparkled in the sunshine, but, lower down, the green meadows were filled with bright spring flowers. Standing on the shore of the lake was a picturesque wooden cabin and Gustav parked in front of it.

'Where are we? Why have you brought me here?' Arielle asked when he opened the door and she got out of the car, followed by Maks.

'Prince Eirik instructed me to drive you to his mountain lodge. It is his private retreat, and he will join you later.'

'But I don't want to stay here.' She followed Gustav inside and tried not to fall in love with the cabin's rustic charm. Colourful rugs on the floors and cosy throws and overstuffed cushions on the sofas gave a homely feel to the place. She poked her head round a door and discovered a bright kitchen with a sturdy-looking oak table.

'I follow the Prince's orders,' Gustav told her. 'The lodge is fully equipped with everything you might need, and there is food in the larder and freezer. Maks will stay with you.'

'I want to speak to Prince Eirik.' Arielle took her phone out of her bag. 'Will you give me his phone number?'

'The Prince cannot be disturbed while he is carrying out royal duties.' Gustav sounded shocked. 'Unfortunately, the mobile phone signal is poor up here.'

Gustav was right, Arielle discovered when she walked around the cabin, trying to get a connection. She heard the car's engine and ran outside to see Eirik's private secretary driving away.

It was not the worst place to be stranded, she conceded when she wandered down to the lake, accompanied by the faithful Maks. The lake was not heated by geothermal activity and was too cold to swim in without a wetsuit. The mountain scenery was breathtaking, but the idea of Eirik spending time in this remote and tranquil place where there wasn't a nightclub or casino anywhere nearby did not fit with his image in the media of a playboy prince.

After a while, Arielle returned to the cabin and rooted through the well-stocked freezer for something to defrost for dinner. Although she hoped Eirik would arrive soon, and she'd insist that he took her back to her flat at the institute. She could not understand why he had sent her to the mountains. Recalling that he had said he wasn't ready to end whatever was between them made her wonder if he wanted to spend another night with her. She bit her lip. Sex with him had been earth-shattering, but while Eirik might not have a problem separating lust from deeper feelings, Arielle wasn't confident that she could do the same.

Lunch was crackers and dried apricots from the larder, and she opened a tin of dog food for Maks. Eirik kept a good selection of books at the cabin. She chose a thriller that had earned rave reviews and quickly became absorbed in the plot. When the sun slipped behind the mountain and the temperature dropped, she lit the log burner. Another hour passed and there was still no word from Eirik. Even if he had sent her a message, the lack of phone signal meant that she hadn't received it.

How dared he abandon her miles from civilisation? Arielle felt powerless, and it was a painful reminder of how she had felt growing up under her father's control. As a child and even when she'd become an adult, she had felt voiceless. Her father had treated her like a skivvy, and at school her shyness had meant that she had been mostly unnoticed by the teachers.

Now Eirik had taken control of her life. She had no way of leaving his mountain retreat and she was effectively a prisoner until he decided to release her. Even if she shouted at the top of her voice, there was no one around to hear her. Growing more furious by the minute, Arielle yanked open the front door and stepped outside. The moon was hidden behind clouds and the darkness was impenetrable.

'Can anyone hear me?' she yelled.

The silence reinforced her sense of unimportance. Blinking back tears, she went back inside. At least nobody had witnessed her being a self-pitying idiot, she told Maks when he nudged her with his damp nose.

Another few hours passed, and she guessed that Eirik was not going to arrive, and she would be spending the night in the cabin with only his dog for company. Deciding that she might as well try to sleep, she changed into her nightdress. The vintage cotton chemise was pretty but impractical on a chilly night, and she wrapped a soft woollen blanket around her before curling up on the sofa in front of the fire.

She must have dozed off, and stirred when Maks got up and padded over to the door. Arielle heard a noise from outside and was instantly on her guard. There had been many nights at the cliff-top cottage when she'd heard strangers' voices downstairs, and she had hidden beneath the bed covers. 'Keep your nose out of my business,' her father had told her, the only time she'd dared to ask him who the visitors were. Automatically she lifted her hand and traced the small scar beneath her left eye.

The door handle began to turn. Heart thumping with fear, she realised that she might need to defend herself and grabbed the fire tongs. The door opened and Maks gave a delighted bark when Eirik walked into the cabin. He smelled of frosty air and sandalwood cologne, and Arielle melted at the sight of him, looking utterly devastating in black jeans and a thick cream sweater.

She dropped the tongs so that she wasn't tempted to use them on him. Her pulse pounded with anger and adrenalin as Eirik strolled towards her. His lazy smile was the bitter end, as was his murmured greeting, 'Hey, baby.'

'You've got a nerve,' she told him heatedly.

His brows lifted. 'Is there a problem?'

'The fact that you have to ask if there's a problem makes the problem even worse.' The words tumbled from her lips as her temper exploded.

He held up his hand. 'If we are going to have a disagreement, can I just say that I will find it impossible to argue with you while you remind me of a fluffy chick?'

'Damn you, Eirik,' she choked out, fighting her way out of the cashmere blanket. 'You had no right to order your servant to dump me in the middle of nowhere.'

His eyes narrowed. 'I asked Gustav to bring you to the cabin—'

'But you didn't ask me if I wanted to visit your mountain retreat,' Arielle cut him off.

He frowned. 'I wasn't sure you would agree to come.'

'So you had me kidnapped and brought here against my will.'

'*Faen!* That's a little dramatic.' Eirik ran his fingers through his hair. 'Listen—'

'No.' She marched over to him and poked her finger in his chest. Hard. 'You listen to me.' She was determined never to be voiceless again, and she refused to be cowed by the angry glitter in Eirik's eyes.

'You made an arbitrary decision without consulting me, and without considering the impact on my career. It must look terrible that I failed to show up at the marine research institute today. I tried calling Valdemar to explain why I wasn't at work, but I couldn't get a phone signal.' She huffed out a breath. 'Valdemar has enough to worry about with Frida's pregnancy. He needs to know that he can rely on me to do my job.'

'He would not have expected you at work because today is a national holiday,' Eirik said calmly.

'Oh.' Arielle remembered that Valdemar had said the day after the masquerade ball was a national holiday, and she could enjoy a couple of glasses of champagne at the party as she wouldn't have to get up early for work.

'Tomorrow is the weekend, and Monday is also a national holiday. I managed to clear my diary so that we can spend a couple of days together.' Eirik grimaced. 'I'd intended to meet you at the cabin much earlier, but my mother had organised a surprise birthday dinner for me, and I couldn't get away.'

Arielle bit her lip. 'I'd forgotten about your birthday. But it doesn't change the fact that you took away my choice of if I wanted to see you again. You think you can do as you please because you are a prince, and I am nobody.'

He frowned. 'I don't think you are nobody.'

'It's how you make me feel. You had me smuggled out of the palace and brought to your remote mountain hideaway. I guess it's because you think I am only good enough for a secret romp. Was Ida Lundberg at your birthday dinner?' Jealousy twisted in Arielle's stomach.

Eirik strode over to a cabinet and took out a bottle of malt whisky. He half filled two glasses and came back to hand her one. Arielle took a sip of the drink and coughed as the fiery spirit hit the back of her throat.

'No, Ida wasn't there,' he said. 'My mother's latest selection of women who could be my wife included an English debutante. As a matter of fact, Lady Laura Hammett comes from your part of the world. Her father has a country house and estate near Truro.'

'Earl Hammett owns a large chunk of Cornwall,' Arielle muttered. 'I'm sure Lady Laura would be a perfect wife and Princess Consort for you.'

Eirik lifted his glass to his lips and gulped down the whisky as if he needed it. 'I'm not interested in Laura or any other woman.' His rough voice sent a prickle across Arielle's skin. Her heart started to pound when he took her glass out of her fingers and set it down next to his on the coffee table. 'I am only interested in you.'

He slid his hand round to her nape and pulled her towards him. Her sensible self knew she should try to resist his potency, but her body responded to him of its own accord and the tingle in her nipples arced down to the molten place between her thighs.

'I thought one night with you would be enough, but I was wrong.' There was frustration in his voice. 'We are highly sexually compatible. That's all this is.' He sounded as if he was trying to convince himself. 'But I can't look at another woman, let alone choose a wife, while I am hungry for you.'

Eirik's admission that he desired her more than any of the sophisticated socialites his mother had lined up as his prospective bride made Arielle's heart flip. He wanted to spend the weekend with her, and she couldn't deny it was what she wanted too. She could not stop thinking about how he had made love to her with fierce passion coupled with infinite patience that had allowed her to explore her sensuality.

When he lowered his head so that his mouth was centimetres away from hers, she waited in anticipation for his kiss. But he pulled back, and maybe her disappointment showed on her face because he said gruffly, 'Before we take this any further, I must warn you not to fall in love with me.'

Did he think she was that much of a fool? Arielle took a deep breath and counted to ten. 'You are going to need a bigger cabin for your ego.'

For a moment Eirik stared at her in a stunned silence, and then he thew back his head and laughed so hard that his shoulders shook. 'I've never met anyone like you,' he told her. 'You are not afraid to say what you think.' His expression became serious.

'That's the first time I've felt like laughing since my brother died.' He reached out and threaded his fingers through her curls. 'At the risk of being shot down in flames, I have to say that you are even more beautiful when you're angry.'

'I've never lost my temper before,' Arielle admitted. Fear of her father's unpredictable moods had meant that she'd supressed her emotions. Even when her mother had died, she'd cried alone in her room after Gerran had told her to stop snivelling. The only time she had stood up to her father had resulted in the scar on her face, and it had been a permanent reminder of his control.

But Arielle was not afraid of Eirik, and she knew he would never harm her physically. Her heart was another matter, but it was up to her to keep her emotions out of the sex-only relationship he wanted. Trusting him had allowed her to voice her anger for the first time in her life, and it felt liberating. What else could Eirik teach her about herself? Arielle wondered. She was eager to find out and gave a low moan when he dipped his head again and this time claimed her mouth in a searing kiss that turned her bones to liquid.

'I don't want to be accused of denying you your right to choose,' he murmured in her ear before he nipped her tender lobe with his teeth. 'You get to decide if you want to make love here on the rug in front of the fire, or in bed.'

'Here first, and then the bed.' She slid her hands beneath his sweater and explored the hard ridges of his abs before opening the zip on his jeans. 'And after that…' She hesitated.

Eirik's brows rose. 'Go on,' he prompted thickly.

'Well… I've fantasised about having sex on the kitchen table,' Arielle confessed, blushing hotly. But she felt emboldened by the gleam in Eirik's eyes to tell him what she wanted.

How the hell was he going to survive this woman? Eirik wondered. Arielle's intriguing mix of naivety and sensuality blew his mind. He was relieved that she understood sex was all there could be between them. Now that he'd established the necessary boundaries, he could relax and enjoy a brief fling with her. Although relaxed was the opposite of how he was feeling right now, he acknowledged, as he pulled his sweater over his head and hauled her close so that the hard points of her nipples pressed against his chest.

His heart thudded as he slid the straps of her lacy nightgown over her shoulders. The row of tiny buttons down the front tested his patience, but he resisted the urge to tear the gown off so that he could get his hands on her naked body. Instead, he concentrated on unwrapping the best birthday present he could have wished for. When the nightgown slid to the floor, he cupped Arielle's breasts in his hands and played with her nipples, eliciting husky moans from her.

Desire was a pagan drumbeat in his blood. He set her away from him and watched the firelight caress her gorgeous curves while he stripped off the rest of his clothes. He was already aroused, and Arielle's swiftly indrawn breath when she saw his proud erection heightened his anticipation.

Her lips parted beneath his as he kissed her deeply. 'Wrap your legs around me,' he bade her, and then he lowered her to the floor and came down beside her.

He knew her body so well, knew what she liked, and he pushed her legs apart and settled his shoulders between her thighs. He skimmed his fingers over the neat vee of red curls that hid her femininity and breathed in the erotic scent of her arousal. 'I want to taste you,' he said hoarsely before he flicked the tip of his tongue along her opening. With his finger he gently parted her, and then used his mouth to give her the most intimate caress of all.

'That feels so good.' Arielle gasped. She tilted her hips to offer herself to him. Eirik was tempted to give her an orgasm with his tongue, but the pressure was building inside him, and he knelt up to roll a condom over his erection and then slid his hands beneath her bottom. He entered her with a smooth thrust and groaned as he pushed deeper into her velvet heat.

'Does this feel good? It does for me. You drive me insane, *skatta*.' Sex had never been so intense with his previous lovers, and his self-control had never been threatened the way it was with Arielle. Eirik started to move, and everything got a whole lot worse, or better, as she matched his rhythm, and he knew he could not hold out for much longer. Their bodies had learned each other's secrets and they moved together in a synchronised dance as sensation built on sensation. His jaw clenched as he fought to hold back the tsunami and drove into her with powerful strokes.

'Eirik,' she cried out as she shuddered beneath him. He covered her mouth with his and kissed her hungrily, thrusting his tongue between her lips as simultaneously he thrust into her body and was overwhelmed by the strongest climax he'd ever experienced. The force of his release tore the breath from his lungs. He slumped on top of her and pressed his lips to her slender neck. After a few minutes he reluctantly lifted himself off her and rolled onto his back, waiting for his heart rate to return to normal.

It was just amazing sex, Eirik assured himself. The intense attraction he felt for Arielle couldn't last. It would burn out—at least he hoped it would. But until then…

He reached for her and drew her down on top of him, refusing to acknowledge the odd clench his heart gave when her body fitted against his as if she had been designed solely for him.

# CHAPTER NINE

'Do you ski on the mountain in winter?'

Eirik stretched luxuriously and opened his eyes to see Arielle sitting up in bed. The window faced the mountain known locally as Kaempen—or Giant. In the gathering dusk, the mountain was a craggy, grey shadow with a dusting of snow on it topmost flanks.

'No, the terrain is not good. Fjernland's only ski resort is a few miles from here.'

'Is that where you and your brother were skiing when there was an avalanche?'

Eirik sat up and leaned back against the headboard. It was Sunday afternoon, and they had barely left the bedroom all weekend other than to raid the kitchen when the need for food had briefly topped their hunger for each other. Arielle had made pancakes served with lingonberry jam and they had fed each other the sweet treat before Eirik had lifted her onto the wooden table and pushed her legs apart to feast on her.

'We were in the French Alps,' he told her. 'Staying at a resort that we had visited years ago. Niels was keen to go back there when I'd suggested a skiing trip.' Eirik exhaled heavily. 'The conditions on the day of the accident were excellent for skiing and there were no indications that an avalanche might occur.'

His mind replayed the shocking moment when he'd glanced over his shoulder and seen a massive wave of snow thundering down the slope. Since then, he had only spoken about his brother with Niels's fiancée, Princess Catalina, when they had grieved together for the man they had both loved. But in the past two days, when he hadn't been having incredible sex with Arielle, they had talked about all manner of things, and he'd found himself opening up to her.

'Niels was the better skier out of the two of us,' he told her. 'From when we were teenagers, my passion was sailing, and I preferred to be on a boat than on the slopes.' His jaw clenched. 'It makes no sense that Niels was killed, and I survived. It should have been the other way round.'

'There was nothing you could have done to prevent the avalanche,' Arielle said quietly. 'Just as I couldn't have stopped my mum from being swept away by a freak wave. Fate can be cruel.'

Eirik reached out and wound a silky red curl around his finger. 'I assumed that your mother had been ill. I didn't realise she died in an accident. You were only young, weren't you?'

'Eleven. It was in the summer before I started secondary school. Mum and I had gone for a swim in the sea. She was a very good swimmer, and a qualified lifeguard. The weather had been calm when we'd swum round the headland to do some snorkelling. But the wind blew up suddenly and a huge wave rolled in. Mum pushed me up onto a ledge on the cliff, but as she tried to climb after me, the wave swept her away.'

Eirik cursed softly and shifted across the bed to draw Arielle against his chest. 'That must have been horrific.'

'It was so quick,' she said in a low voice. 'One second Mum was there, and in the next she had disappeared before my eyes.'

'I know what you mean. I watched my brother try to outrun the avalanche and then he was gone, buried beneath tons of snow. I prayed for the only time in my life,' Eirik admitted rawly. 'I prayed that Niels would be found alive. I couldn't accept that he was dead until his body was found three days later.'

He could only imagine how traumatised Arielle had been when she'd seen her mother swept away by a giant wave. He tightened his arms around her, wishing he could shield her from painful memories.

'I felt guilty that I hadn't jumped into the sea to help Mum. I suppose I was in a state of shock, and I clung to the rocks until I was spotted by some people on a boat, who rescued me.'

Eirik tilted Arielle's face up and felt a tug in his chest when he saw tears clinging to her eyelashes. 'There was nothing you could have done to save your mother. You must believe that.'

She nodded. 'Just as you could not have skied

uphill and snatched your brother from the path of the avalanche.'

'I know,' he muttered. 'I felt so helpless. After Niels died, I felt guilty for being alive. My brother was not only the better skier, but he was also the better son, and he would have been a better Sovereign than me.'

'You can't think that. It's not true.' Arielle's voice was fierce, and she stared at him intently as if she was willing him to believe her. She laid her hand on his jaw, and Eirik turned his head and kissed her palm.

'Thank you,' he said gruffly. If he was fighting a battle, he would want Arielle by his side, he brooded.

'Sometimes things happen that are beyond our control,' she murmured.

Like getting more involved with Arielle than he had intended. Eirik's jaw tightened. He had lost count of how many times he had made love to her, and it was always, impossibly, better than the time before. Their sexual compatibility was off the scale. But there was more. He liked her, which was a first for him. In the past, personality had come at the bottom of the list of attributes he'd looked for in his lovers. Sexual attraction had invariably led to a brief affair, or more often a one-night stand before he'd moved on to the next pretty woman who had caught his eye.

This was different. For a start he wanted to know everything about Arielle, and he felt protective of her. He had brought her to Fjernland after her studio had been vandalised, but he could have sent a couple of his security team to her cottage to keep an eye on her. It was odd how she had been adamant that she did not want to report the break-in to the police, Eirik remembered.

Arielle rested her head on his shoulder. 'Mum's body was never found. Search and rescue teams looked for days, but it was likely that she had been swept out to sea by the strong current.'

'How is it that you love to swim in the sea after your mother drowned? You risked your life to save mine.' Her bravery was even more astonishing now he knew what she had witnessed as a child. 'I would have expected you to be scared of the power of the ocean.'

Her sweet smile made Eirik want to protect her from all of life's hurts. 'Mum believed that mermaids exist and maybe she was right,' she said softly. 'When I free-dive wearing my monofin I feel close to her.'

He brushed his lips over her hair. 'What about your father? You haven't mentioned him.'

She stiffened and pulled out of his arms. 'I'd rather not talk about him,' Arielle said abruptly. 'It's...difficult.'

Eirik vaguely recalled that she might have told him both of her parents were dead. Perhaps she had lost her father recently and found it too painful to speak about him.

He frowned. Why did he feel frustrated and hurt, dammit, because Arielle had shut him out? He moved down the bed and settled her on top of him. Framing her lovely face with his hands, he kissed the tip of her nose. Her skin was flawless apart from the tiny scar beneath her left eye. 'How did you get this?' he asked softly, brushing his thumb pad over the mark.

Once again, she tensed and avoided his gaze. 'Oh, it happened years ago. I…um…tripped and banged my face against the corner of the table.'

Arielle pushed herself upright so that she was sitting astride him and circled her pelvis against his. The effect was instantaneous, and Eirik felt himself harden. 'I can think of more enjoyable things to do in bed than talk,' she murmured seductively.

He let her take the lead and groaned when she guided herself down onto him, taking his throbbing erection deep insider her. With her fiery curls flying around her shoulders and her green eyes darkened to mysterious pools, she was utterly irresistible as she rode him to another mind-blowing climax. But afterwards, while their limbs were still tangled and their breathing was fractured, Eirik wondered why Arielle had lied about the scar on her cheek.

The weather, like Arielle's mood, had turned dismal. Rain lashed the promenade next to the beach, and the car splashed through puddles when Eirik turned into the courtyard in front of the Fjernland Marine Research Institute. It was Tuesday morning after the extended weekend, and they had left the mountain cabin early so that she could be at the institute in time for work. Conversation during the journey to the coast had been stilted. Eirik seemed to be absorbed in his own thoughts, and even Maks was subdued and lay on the back seat with his head between his paws.

'I have a feeling of déjà vu,' Arielle muttered when Eirik pulled into a parking bay, and they watched the rain beating against the windscreen. 'You dropped me off at the institute two and a half weeks ago, and I wished you luck in your search for a wife.'

He scowled at her flippant tone. Arielle refused to let him guess that her heart felt as fragile as spun glass. 'It is my duty to marry,' he said curtly.

'What would happen if you didn't get married and have a son and heir?' Her common sense told her to drop the subject and walk away from him with her dignity intact, but she seemed to be glued to the passenger seat.

'The heir to the throne does not have to be male,' he surprised her by saying. 'If my firstborn child is a daughter she will be the future Sovereign.'

Arielle pictured Eirik holding a little girl with blonde hair and blue eyes the colour of summer skies. If he married Ida Lundberg they would have beautiful children, she thought, feeling a pang of envy.

'To answer your question,' he continued. 'If I did not have a legitimate heir to ascend the throne after me, then, under the rules of the constitution, Fjernland would become a protectorate of Denmark. To put it simply, Fjernland would no longer be a principality and would lose its independent status that it gained in the tenth century.'

Eirik ran his hand over the stubble on his jaw. He hadn't trimmed his beard for a few days and looked rakishly handsome. 'A recent poll showed that ninety-eight per cent of the population want to be ruled by the monarchy. I will not let my parents down, or fail the Fjernlandic people,' he said tautly.

The rain had eased off a little, and Eirik retrieved Arielle's bag from the boot of the car before coming round to open her door. 'Wait there,' he told Maks. Arielle saw that he had left the window partly open for the dog's comfort.

The empty car park was a sign that the marine scientists and other staff who worked at the institute had not arrived yet. They walked over to the accommodation block and took the lift up to the third floor. Arielle's tension grew when Eirik followed her into her apartment. He was prolonging the inevitable when he would leave. It was unlikely she would meet him again, but no doubt his wedding to whichever aristocratic woman he decided to marry would be shown on TV and be headline news around the world.

She watched him prowl around her small but functional flat. 'I need to get ready for work,' she reminded him. 'Thanks for a nice weekend.'

His brows rose. 'Nice! Seriously, is that all it was for you?'

She glared at him. 'Do you want me to thank you for the most amazing sex I've ever had?'

'It was amazing for me too.' Eirik's soft tone made inroads on her heart. 'Come with me. I want to show you something. It won't take long.'

With a sigh, she followed him back to the lift and they went up to the top floor of the building.

'This is incredible,' Arielle murmured when Eirik ushered her into a huge open-plan apartment. Floor-to-ceiling windows along an entire wall gave a panoramic view of the beach, which even on a grey day was wild and beautiful. The décor in the apartment was Scandi style, with pale wood floors, and walls and furniture in neutral tones. Minimalism combined with comfort that probably cost a fortune, Arielle thought.

'I had the penthouse designed when I established the marine research institute,' Eirik told her. 'I lived here when I ran my yacht-building business, but now I've sold the business and I am busy with royal duties the penthouse is empty most of the time.' He strolled over to her and caught hold of her hand, linking his fingers through hers. 'You could move in here.'

Her eyes widened. 'Me? Why? I have an apartment. It's not as impressive as this, but I doubt I'd be able to afford the rent for the penthouse.'

Eirik pulled her towards him, and Arielle went unresistingly because it might be the last time she was in his arms. 'Don't worry about the rent,' he murmured. 'If you live at the penthouse I will be able to visit you without anyone knowing of our involvement.'

Arielle's heart dropped into the pit of her stomach. 'Are you suggesting that I could be your secret mistress?'

His eyes blazed. 'We are good together, *skatta.*

You admitted that it was the best sex you've ever had. And it's the same for me. I don't want to lose you.'

Her emotions see-sawed. Eirik seemed to be saying that he wanted her in his life, but she would be his grubby secret. They would not have a relationship, just an involvement, which was another way of saying he wanted to have sex with her when it was convenient for him to visit her at the penthouse. Arielle remembered Eirik had said that when he was growing up he hadn't had a close relationship with his parents, particularly his mother, who had largely ignored him while she'd desperately tried to win Prince Otto's love. Maybe being starved of affection in his childhood had hardened his heart and it was why he shunned emotional relationships.

'But you must marry soon so that your father can abdicate, and you will become the Reigning Sovereign with your Princess Consort to assist you.'

'I am not married at the moment. Even when I become engaged, a wedding will take time to arrange.' He shrugged. 'And afterwards I will retain my freedom.'

Arielle bit her lip. 'How can you ask a woman, perhaps Ida Lundberg, to spend the rest of her life with you when you are not prepared to offer her commitment and fidelity?'

Eirik's jaw tightened. 'I will make it clear to whoever I marry that in public we will give a show of unity, but in private we'll have separate lives, and lovers, as long as we are discreet.'

'That was what your parents' marriage was like,

wasn't it? But you told me that your mother loved your father and was hurt by his affairs. What will you do if your wife falls in love with you?'

He swore. 'It won't happen. But if it did, why would it matter to you?'

'Because you have asked me to be your mistress. I'd be the third person in your marriage, and it would be unbearable to know that I was the reason for your wife's heartbreak.'

Eirik raked his hand through his hair. 'This is a crazy conversation. I don't have a wife.'

*'Yet.'* Arielle let out her breath slowly. 'You need to court the woman you intend to marry and who will be the mother of your children.' She tried to smile but failed. 'Who knows, you might fall in love with your bride.'

'I have neither the desire nor intention to fall in love,' Eirik said curtly. He tightened his arm around Arielle's waist so that she was plastered against his whipcord body, and threaded his other hand into her tangled curls, which she'd meant to style into a neat chignon before starting work in the marine laboratories. She should not be here in his penthouse, and her body should not be responding to the glitter in his eyes as he lowered his face towards hers. 'I want you, and you want me,' he insisted. 'That is all that matters for now.'

His warm breath grazed her lips, and she was so tempted to lose herself in the mastery of his kiss, but somehow she resisted. 'You want to keep me hidden,'

Arielle muttered. 'Are you ashamed of me because I am a nobody?'

Eirik lifted his head and stared down at her. 'Of course I'm not ashamed of you. And you are not a nobody. Why do you put yourself down? You are beautiful, clever, passionate about marine conservation, and as sexy as hell.'

'But you wouldn't ask me out to a restaurant, or anywhere where we could be seen in public. I would be your invisible mistress.'

He frowned. 'Have you any idea what your life would be like if we were spotted together? If there was speculation that we were in a relationship, you would be hounded by the press. I have had to deal with media intrusion in my personal life for as long as I can remember, but you have never experienced the relentless attention you would receive.'

Oh, but she had, and it was an experience she never wanted to repeat. Arielle shuddered at the memory of the pack of journalists and press photographers who had been outside the court during her father's trial. The rumours that she had known about Gerran Rowse's drug-smuggling operation, and the murder of a policeman, had put her in the spotlight three years ago. Even before then, when she was a child, her surly father had been unpopular with the villagers in Penash because of his filthy temper and readiness to start a brawl in the pub when he was drunk. As a consequence, Arielle had been picked on by other children at school simply because she'd been seen as different. After Gerran had been sent to prison, she had been treated with suspicion by the villagers.

If the press in Fjernland discovered that the future monarch was having an affair with the daughter of a notorious criminal, the story would make headline news. Worst of all, Eirik would learn about her past. She had done nothing wrong, but she was deeply ashamed of her connection to her vile father.

Reality hit Arielle like a sledgehammer. She would never agree to be Eirik's mistress once he was married. But while he was still single, she had been tempted to have an affair with him in the hope that the chemistry between them would fizzle out. And if she was honest, she'd hoped that the fairy tale would come true, and the handsome prince would fall in love and want to marry her.

Eirik had made it clear there was no chance of that happening, but if a miracle occurred and he decided to conduct their relationship in the public eye, it would be a nightmare, Arielle realised sickly. The press would be certain to dig up the dirt on her father and she would be humiliated in front of Eirik. Worse still, Eirik would be embarrassed by his association with her, and perhaps his judgement would be questioned by the people of Fjernland. She simply could not allow that to happen.

He slid his hand beneath her chin and tilted her face up to his. 'When I arranged for you to be taken to the cabin without asking if you wanted to go, you accused me of denying you the right to make your own choices. I'm not asking you to decide right now where we go from here.' His eyes blazed. 'But you won't find this fire with anyone else, *skatta*.'

He bent his head and crushed her mouth beneath his in a kiss that startled Arielle with its urgency. She wound her arms around his neck and ran her fingers through the blond hair above his collar. When Eirik kissed her passionately as he was doing and stroked his finger gently over her cheek as if she were infinitely precious, she could almost believe that she meant something to him. But it was hopeless.

She broke the kiss and pulled out of his arms. He did not stop her, and his expression was unreadable. 'I...have to go,' she whispered before she walked quickly over to the door and out of the penthouse.

Valdemar arrived at the marine research institute in the afternoon. He looked as though he hadn't slept for days, but there was a wide grin on his face.

'How is Frida?' Arielle asked him. She really liked the couple and had enjoyed working with Frida on a report about microplastic pollution in the oceans and possible solutions to the problem.

'Mother and baby are doing well.' Valdemar showed her a picture on his phone of a tiny infant swaddled in blankets. 'Meet my son, Lars,' he said with obvious pride. 'The birth had to be induced because of Frida's dangerously high blood pressure and Lars is small because he was a month early. But he has a healthy pair of lungs that he uses particularly well at night.'

'Congratulations.' Arielle felt an unexpected pull

of maternal longing as she looked at the photo of the newborn baby. She'd vaguely hoped she would have a family one day, but she would want to be with a man who loved her and their children. Would Eirik love the heir he must produce to ensure that Fjernland continued to be an independent principality? She hoped so, for she knew what it was like to grow up without a loving father.

'Come into my office,' Valdemar said. He offered Arielle a seat. 'You may remember that Frida was meant to address the National Council and report on the effects of microplastics in the marine environment.'

Arielle nodded. 'We wrote the report together and our findings are based on sediment samples taken from the North Sea.'

'The assembly will take place on Saturday, but Frida is on maternity leave, and we are both agreed that you should address the National Council.'

'But there are other, more highly qualified marine biologists than me who would be better to give the report,' Arielle stammered.

'You demonstrated when you gave a seminar to a group of university students a week ago that you have a gift for public speaking. Also, you wrote the report with Frida, which makes you the ideal person to deliver the speech.' Valdemar smiled. 'Please agree to take Frida's place. A lot is riding on the report, and we are hoping to persuade the National Council to increase the marine research institute's funding.'

'Well... I am honoured that you have chosen me.'

Shocked was a better description of how she felt, Arielle thought. After a lifetime of feeling voiceless, she was being encouraged to make a speech about a subject close to her heart and hopefully bring more attention to marine conservation. It was thanks to Eirik that she had been given this chance. He had brought her to Fjernland to work at the research institute. Why did everything centre around him? she thought with a sigh.

For the rest of the week Arielle worked on polishing the wording of the speech that she would give to the National Council. Valdemar had explained that the fifteen members of the government were elected by the Fjernlandic people every three years, and the ministers assisted the hereditary Reigning Sovereign to rule the principality. Crown Prince Otto was convalescing after his recent illness and Prince Eirik would deputise for his father at the National Council's assembly.

At least worrying about speaking at such a prestigious event had helped to keep her mind off Eirik during the days, Arielle thought ruefully. But she was lonely in bed without him. They had spent four nights together at his cabin in the mountains and she had grown used to curling up against his big body when they were in bed, which had been most of the time. She felt a familiar tingle of longing in her breasts and low in her pelvis as she remembered his skill as a lover. He had taken her to heaven with his thrilling caresses, but he'd coupled fierce passion with an unexpected tenderness that had captivated her heart.

On the first night back in her flat she had still been awake at midnight when her phone rang and Eirik's name flashed on the screen.

'I take it you can't sleep either,' he'd drawled when she'd answered on the second ring.

'No,' she'd admitted.

'I miss you.' His husky voice had made her toes curl.

'I miss you too.'

'Good. Tell me what you have been doing.'

She had told him about the report she'd been asked to give at the National Council's assembly. It had led to a wider discussion about marine conservation and Eirik's determination to protect Fjernland's seas and the island's unique natural environment when he became the Reigning Sovereign.

'You helped me to realise that when I am the monarch, I will be able to introduce changes to some of the policies that are outdated and hopefully bring a new energy to how Fjernland is governed,' he'd told her. 'I have made my peace with the royal life and responsibilities that await me.'

'I'm glad,' Arielle had said. She'd wondered if Eirik had also accepted that marriage was a non-negotiable part of his royal life. He did not mention *their* relationship and perhaps he had decided to take her advice and court the woman he planned to make his bride.

He had phoned again last night, and they had

chatted until two a.m. When her alarm had gone off at six, she had struggled to wake up. After work she visited Valdemar and Frida and admired baby Lars. Arielle had never held a tiny baby before, and when she walked back to her apartment block next to the institute, she thought wistfully of the Oskarssons' happy family unit.

The sight of a black limousine in the car park made her heart leap at the thought that Eirik was here and would invite her up to his penthouse. As she approached the car, the chauffeur held the rear door open. Eirik must be intending to take her somewhere, Arielle thought as she slid onto the back seat.

'Hi, gorgeous…' Her voice faltered as her eyes met Princess Hulda's icy gaze. 'G-good afternoon, Your Highness. I did not realise…'

'I assume you were expecting to see my son, Miss Tremain. Or should I address you as Miss Rowse? That is the name recorded on your birth certificate.'

Nausea churned in Arielle's stomach. 'I…'

'You changed your name to Tremain, which was your mother's maiden name, after your father, Gerran Rowse, was convicted of murder and sent to prison.'

'H-how did you find out?'

'At a dinner party I gave for Prince Eirik's birthday, I happened to mention you to one of the guests whose family are landowners in the south-west of England. Lady Laura Hammett recognised the name Arielle, but she thought your surname was Rowse. Your father had the dubious distinction of being Cornwall's most notorious drug dealer until his criminal activities were exposed when he shot and killed a police officer who had been investigating his illegal activities.'

'Does Eirik know?' Arielle whispered.

Princess Hulda arched her brows. 'So, you have not told my son about your family background. I rather thought you would not have done. But it was possible that you had convinced Eirik you were unaware of your father's crimes.'

'I *was* unaware…'

The Princess held up her hand imperiously, and Arielle fell silent. 'It is Prince Eirik's duty to marry a high-born woman who will be the Princess Consort. You mean nothing to him.' She gave a humourless laugh. 'Eirik has always allowed his urges to override his judgement. It is time that his dalliance with you finished.' The Princess's curiously colourless eyes raked over Arielle's ashen face. 'I suggest that you end your affair with the heir to the throne and leave Fjernland, Miss Rowse. There is no reason for you to remain here. Secrets rarely stay secret for ever.' Princess Hulda's lethally soft voice felt like a knife through Arielle's heart.

She swallowed. 'Are you blackmailing me?'

The cold eyes flicked towards her. 'I will do whatever is necessary to ensure the continuation of Fjernland's monarchy.'

'Even if it means pressurising Eirik into a loveless marriage?'

'Ah, you are in love with the Prince.'

'N-no.' Arielle frantically denied it to the Princess and herself.

'And you hope that my son might fall in love with you? Let us suppose he did.' Princess Hulda tapped her fingernails on the leather armrest. 'The Fjernlandic people would not accept a criminal's daughter as the Princess Consort. If you had a child with Eirik, the future heir to the throne would share the bloodline of a murderer.'

Arielle drew a sharp breath. She felt tainted by her father's crimes, but far worse was the realisation that any children she might have would carry the same burden of shame. Eirik's mother had said that secrets rarely stayed secret for ever, and it was true. The story was bound to crop up from time to time, or feature on one of those true crime programmes that were so popular. She would never escape her association with a cold-blooded killer.

Princess Hulda tapped on the privacy screen, and the chauffeur got out of the car and opened the rear door for Arielle. 'Goodbye, Miss Rowse,' the Princess said briskly. 'I do not anticipate that we will meet again.'

As Arielle let herself into her flat, her phone rang. She stared at Eirik's name before she dropped the phone and ran to the bathroom to be violently sick. Staggering into the living room, she shoved her phone under a pile of cushions when it rang again. The third time Eirik called, she switched her phone off and curled up in a ball on the sofa. Her body was icy cold and hot tears streamed down her face.

# CHAPTER TEN

EIRIK KNOTTED HIS grey silk tie before he slipped his waistcoat on. His valet held out his suit jacket for him to slide his arms into the sleeves. 'That will be all, thank you, Mikkel,' he murmured.

His phone was on the table in his dressing room and the ping of a new message arriving had him stride across the room and snatch up the device. Disappointment left a bitter taste in his mouth when he saw that the text was not from Arielle. Since they had returned from his cabin in the mountains three days ago, he had not been free to see her, but he'd looked forward to their nightly phone conversations. However, when he'd called her yesterday she had not answered. He'd left numerous messages, asking her to get in touch, but she hadn't responded. He looked at the last text he had sent her.

Miss you. Please call me.

Eirik swore and shoved his phone into his pocket. He was behaving like a lovesick teenager, but he couldn't stop thinking about Arielle and wondering why she had cut off communication with him. Guiltily, he remembered how in the past he'd stopped taking calls from his ex-lovers when they hadn't wanted to accept that the affair was over.

He reminded himself that the speech Arielle was due to give to the National Council tomorrow was a big deal to her, and it was likely she wanted to focus on preparing her report.

His private secretary was pacing up and down the carpet when Eirik walked into the sitting room of his private apartment in Sejrrig Palace.

'Sir, you need to see this.' Gustav's usually calm demeanour was missing, and he looked rattled as he held out a newspaper.

Without a word Eirik took it and stared in shock and mounting fury at the picture on the front page, of him and Ida Lundberg in what looked to be a close embrace. In the photograph, Eirik had his arm around Ida's waist, and her body was turned into his. Her head was tilted towards him while his cheek rested against hers. It was difficult to tell from the angle of the shot, but they appeared to be kissing. The headline on the paper said *Royal Betrothal Announcement Expected Within Hours!*

Eirik's first thought was that the photo was a fake. With modern technology it was easy to create an image that looked genuine. But as he studied the picture, he recognised that it had been taken the previous day, outside an art gallery that he had visited in his role as Patron of the Arts. He was meant to have been accompanied by Princess Hulda, but at the last minute she had suffered a migraine and had sent her lady-in-waiting to take her place.

'As you can imagine, the picture is all over social media sites,' Gustav told him.

There had been literally hundreds of messages on Eirik's phone, but he hadn't bothered to look at them when he'd seen that none were from Arielle. Now he remembered that when he had emerged from the art gallery Ida had been beside him. She had stumbled as she'd walked down the steps, and Eirik had reacted automatically and wrapped his arm around her waist to prevent her from falling. For a few seconds as Ida had regained her balance, her body had been plastered against his, and he'd felt nothing. She was an attractive young woman, but his libido had not shown the slightest interest.

The incident had been so brief that he had forgotten it. Camera flashbulbs had been going off, but he hadn't considered how damaging a photo of him and Ida would look. Had it been a genuine accident when she'd tripped on the steps? Eirik swore. He suspected that his mother and Ida had hatched the plan, which they'd believed would force him into marriage. His mother did not suffer from migraine attacks. And if she had actually been unwell, surely she would have kept her lady-in-waiting at the palace to attend to her.

'I was set up,' he muttered.

'Princess Hulda is in her sitting room and wishes to see you urgently,' Gustav informed him.

'I bet she does.' Eirik gritted his teeth. 'I've played right into my mother's hands.'

He wondered if Arielle had seen the newspaper picture or the frenzied rumours on social media that his engagement to Ida was imminent. Would she think that he had taken her advice to court Ida before marrying her? He frowned. Arielle had stopped taking his phone calls before the photograph had been published.

The one thing Eirik was absolutely certain of was that he could not marry Ida Lundberg. He had told Arielle that love would not be a requirement when he married, and he'd meant it. But Arielle had reminded him that his wife would be the mother of his children. He realised that he wanted friendship and even affection between him and the woman he married. Otherwise, their children would grow up in a tense and unhappy family as he and his brother had done.

'Tell Princess Hulda that I will be with her in half an hour,' he instructed Gustav. 'And ask Miss Lundberg to meet me in the library immediately.'

'I have arranged a press briefing this morning so that you can make a formal announcement of your engagement to Ida. What do you think about holding the wedding in early July? It will give enough time for all the arrangements to be made. Your father is preparing to abdicate as monarch at the beginning of September when you will succeed him with your Princess Consort by your side.' Princess Hulda finally ran out of steam and looked expectantly at her son. 'Why are you glowering at me, Eirik? Do you have nothing to say?'

'Oh, I have plenty to say, Mama, but I will spare your sensitivities.' Eirik strode past the sofa where his mother was sitting in front of a low table that held a tea tray. He was not in the mood for a tea party. 'I will not be marrying Ida in July or any other time. At the press briefing I'll explain that there has been a misunderstanding and the rumours that we are engaged are untrue.'

The Princess slammed the teapot down. 'It is your duty to marry her now that a photograph of the two of you has appeared on the front page of every newspaper. Your behaviour has compromised Ida's reputation.'

'My behaviour? Your own behaviour does not bear close scrutiny,' he grated. 'Ida admitted to me that you persuaded her to carry out her little stunt yesterday.'

Eirik pushed his hands into his trouser pockets. He felt restless and stifled in his mother's over-fussy sitting room. He thought longingly of his mountain cabin, the big skies and sense of freedom, and Arielle. She was always in his mind.

'I have told Ida that I have no intention of marrying her and apologised if I did anything that led her to believe I was considering making her my wife.' Eirik sighed when he saw his mother's pinched expression. 'I give you my word that I will marry, but you must allow me to choose my bride when I am ready.'

* * *

Arielle felt a nervous wreck whenever she remembered—and she was not likely to forget—that the National Council's assembly was tomorrow. She had edited her report to within an inch of its life, and Frida had read it and said that it was perfect. But the prospect of standing on a podium in front of government ministers, aides and goodness knew who else was terrifying. The knowledge that Eirik would also attend the assembly and perhaps be accompanied by his new fiancée made things even worse.

Ever since Arielle had seen the photo that was all over social media of Eirik and Ida wrapped around each other while they appeared to be kissing, she had switched off her phone and avoided watching TV. There were rumours of a summer royal wedding, but she would have left Fjernland long before then. She planned to give her resignation letter to Valdemar after she'd delivered her speech. He and Frida had become good friends and she'd miss them as much as she would miss working at the marine research institute.

Arielle sighed as she climbed out of the bath and dried herself on a towel before pulling on her fluffy pink dressing gown. Eirik's mother had been right to guess that she was in love with him. Deeply, madly in love. And feeling the way she did meant that it would be unbearable to remain in Fjernland. She hoped for Eirik's sake that his marriage to Ida would be happy. But he had said that he would retain his freedom after he married, and if he asked her to be his secret mistress, he would break her heart irreparably.

She frowned when there was a knock on the front door. Her neighbour in the apartment block often asked to borrow milk or coffee. But when she opened the door, her heart crashed into her ribs. Eirik lounged in the doorway, looking diabolically handsome in jeans and a black fine-knit sweater that moulded his muscular torso.

'Shouldn't you be with your fiancée?' Arielle muttered. 'I thought your mother would be over the moon about your engagement to Ida Lundberg and give a dinner party in honour of the happy couple.' She could not prevent a note of bitterness in her voice.

Eirik's eyes narrowed to gleaming blue slits. 'Evidently you have not kept up to speed with the news reports. I am not engaged. I have told Ida that there is no chance of us marrying.'

Arielle was so shocked that she simply stared at him. 'Was Ida upset?' she finally asked.

'Disappointed that she won't be a princess, but she acknowledged that if we had married, it would have been a disaster. There is no spark of attraction between us.' Eirik reached out and caught a handful of Arielle's curls. 'Unlike between you and me,' he murmured. 'Our sexual chemistry is more than a spark, it's a wildfire.'

Her breath was trapped in her lungs. 'You don't want to marry me,' she choked out, reminding herself that Eirik would never choose her to be his princess. But supposing he *had* decided to marry her instead of Ida…?

'Of course not,' he said smoothly. 'But we are good together. You know it's true, *skatta*.' He ran his other hand over the front of her dressing gown, and despite the thick material her nipples tautened. 'Even when you're dressed like a pink marshmallow you turn me on more than any woman ever has.' Eirik linked his fingers through hers and brought her hand up to his lips. 'Come up to the penthouse with me.'

'I can't.' Temptation and desire were a potent mix that she knew she must resist. A shiver ran through Arielle when she remembered Princess Hulda's threat to tell Eirik about her father. There was a chance that Eirik would feel sympathy for her. After all, she was not responsible for Gerran's crimes. But she still felt ashamed of her background. She dared not succumb to temptation and make love with Eirik when it would break her heart to do so.

'I want to practise reading my report aloud so there are no glitches tomorrow,' she told him.

He moved past her and stepped into the tiny sitting room. 'The conference suite where the National Council assembly is held is about ten times bigger than your entire flat. If you practise your speech in the penthouse it will give you a better idea of the level to pitch your voice. Is this the report?' He picked up the copy of her speech from the coffee table and walked back to the front door.

Arielle sighed as she gave in to her longing to spend one more hour with Eirik. 'I need to get dressed.'

He was already heading down the corridor towards the lift. 'You're fine as you are.'

'I feel ridiculous,' she told him a few minutes later. Eirik had directed her to stand at one end of the penthouse's open-plan living space and he was sitting on a chair at the opposite end of the room. 'Especially in my dressing gown.'

'Take it off,' he suggested.

'I'm not wearing anything beneath it.'

The low growl he made sounded as primitive as a lion's mating call, and molten heat pooled between Arielle's thighs. She cleared her throat and tried to concentrate on reading out her report. The sooner she got on with it, the quicker she could leave the penthouse before her resistance to Eirik's potency crumbled.

After a nervous start, she got into her stride and gave the speech. 'Did I sound okay?' she asked as Eirik stood up and walked towards her.

'You were brilliant. I mean it,' he said when she looked doubtful. 'Your enthusiasm for marine conservation is obvious.' He halted in front of her, and Arielle breathed in the intoxicating scent of his aftershave.

'I should go,' she mumbled. 'I want to get to bed early.'

'It's seven thirty.' His slow smile sent a tremor through her. 'But an early night is an excellent idea.'

'Eirik…' Her half-hearted protest was lost in his kiss as he angled his mouth over hers and teased her lips apart with his tongue. She would not deny herself this one final time to make love with him, Arielle decided, knowing that she was weak, but unable to resist him. Even though he was not going to marry Ida Lundberg, he must choose an aristocratic bride for the sake of the principality he would soon rule. But tonight he was hers. She pushed his mother's threats to the back of her mind. Tonight she would show Eirik with her body what she could not tell him in words.

Eirik lifted her into his arms and carried her through to the bedroom. She rested her head on his shoulder and brushed her lips over his stubbled jaw. He turned his head and their mouths fused in a slow, sensual kiss that left them both breathless.

'You are so beautiful,' he said thickly.

'So are you.' She studied his face to imprint his chiselled cheekbones and the seductive curve of his mouth on her mind.

He set her down on her feet and untied the belt of her dressing gown before he pushed the robe off her shoulders and skimmed his hands over her naked body, finding each pleasure point with his fingers and then his mouth. She moaned when he closed his lips around one nipple and sucked the tender peak before he moved across to her other breast to do the same.

Desire swept hot and urgent through her veins when he slipped his hand between her legs and brushed his thumb over her sensitive upper thigh. Higher he went, until he found her wet heat and pushed his finger inside her. She rocked her hips against his hand, needing more, desperate for him to possess her fully.

Arielle reminded herself that she wanted their last night of lovemaking to be a memorable experience for Eirik. She did not belong in his world, but she was determined he would never forget her. He groaned when she slipped her hands beneath his sweater and roamed them over his chest. She felt the erratic thud of his heart beneath her fingertips and wished she could tell him that her heart belonged to him.

Sadness would come later. Now there was only the brush of skin against skin when he pulled his sweater over his head and drew her close to him. His chest hairs were silky beneath her cheek. She ran his zip down, and he kicked off his jeans and underwear to stand before her, naked and magnificently aroused. In the light from the bedside lamp he was a golden god, her prince. No other man would ever come close to him.

When he pulled her down onto the bed, she leaned over him and scattered kisses over his chest, following the arrowing of dark blond hairs down to his groin where his erection was jutting proudly.

'Do you have any idea what you do to me?' he growled, his thighs tensing as she ran her tongue along his swollen length before taking him into her mouth.

She loved to give him pleasure, and his unsteady breaths emboldened her to become even more inventive with her caresses. Eirik speared his fingers into her hair and shifted his hips restlessly. Having him completely at her mercy evoked a fierce tenderness in Arielle. He was so strong, this man, but she had glimpsed a vulnerability in him that made her love him even more.

Moving back up his body, she clasped his face in her hands and kissed his mouth before she took the condom he'd left on the bedside table and slid it over his manhood.

'Arielle.' He spoke her name like a prayer as he rolled them both over and settled himself between her spread thighs. His eyes blazed with an emotion she dared not try to define. With infinite care he entered her and sank deeper and deeper until he filled her, and they were one.

There was no need for words. Their bodies moved together in an age-old dance, and yet each touch and caress felt new and breathtaking. She arched her hips to meet his thrusts as he set a devastating rhythm and every powerful stroke sent her closer to the edge. He held her there and bent his head to claim her lips in a lingering kiss that was utterly beguiling.

She sensed his urgency and locked her ankles around his hips as he increased his pace and drove into her faster, harder, until they both toppled over the edge. Eirik let out a savage groan and Arielle pressed her lips to his throat and tasted sweat on his skin.

How could something that felt so right be wrong? she wondered. Princess Hulda's coldly condemning expression came into Arielle's mind and reminded her of why she must leave Fjernland.

* * *

She looked good. Arielle did a slow twirl in front of the mirror. The woman who looked back at her was dressed in an elegant dark blue suit. Beneath the buttonless jacket she was wearing a crisp white blouse. Three-quarter-length trousers made the most of her long legs that were further complemented by nude-coloured stiletto-heeled shoes. Her curls had been tamed into a sleek style and she looked professional and self-confident. The soft flush on her cheeks was the only telltale sign that she was a woman in love, and a closer inspection revealed shadows in her eyes.

But no one at the National Council's assembly would guess that her heart was breaking, Arielle told herself as she picked up her handbag and the report she was to give and exited the cloakroom to make her way to the conference suite. She walked to the front of the assembly room and sat on a chair at the side of the dais as an official had instructed her to do. The rows of seats facing the dais quickly filled, and everyone stood up when Prince Eirik strode into the room and walked down the central aisle to take his seat in the front row.

The last time Arielle had seen him, he had been naked and sprawled on the bed at the penthouse, his blond hair falling across his brow and an indolent smile on his lips after they'd enjoyed early morning sex. Now he was impeccably dressed in a light grey suit, and his expression was enigmatic.

Valdemar hurried over to the dais and sat down next to Arielle. 'The baby was sick on my jacket just before I left home,' he said under his breath. 'I wiped off most of it, but I thinks it's left a stain.'

'It's not too bad,' she whispered, trying not to giggle. The flash of normality eased her tension. Valdemar stood and walked to the centre of the dais to explain to the audience about the role of the marine research institute. When he introduced Arielle, she walked up to the lectern and arranged her notes in front of her. She glanced at Eirik, and her heart lifted when he winked at her. Without him, she would not have had the courage to speak in public. He had helped her to find her voice that her father had silenced. Taking a deep breath, she started to speak.

'In summary,' she told the assembly some twenty minutes later, 'the marine research institute needs your support to help in the fight against plastic pollution. Education, advocacy, and science will allow us to start to create changes in consumer and corporate behaviour that will benefit the world's oceans and ecosystems.'

Loud applause rang out in the assembly room when Arielle finished her report. She sensed that she had made a real connection with the audience and felt quietly proud of herself. Valdemar gave her a thumbs-up sign. She looked over at Eirik, but at that moment a commotion at the back of the room made everyone turn their heads.

The doors to the conference room were opened by two security guards and Princess Hulda walked into the room. A sense of foreboding snaked through

Arielle when the Princess directed her haughty gaze at her.

'Arielle,' Valdemar said in a loud whisper from the side of the stage. 'It's time for you to answer questions from the audience.'

She blinked and turned her head to the front, struggling to regain her composure while she frantically wondered what Eirik's mother was doing here. Arielle shot a lightning glance at Eirik and guessed from his frown that he was surprised by his mother's appearance at the National Council's assembly.

One of the council members asked for more details about her proposal to encourage schools to organise beach-clean events for their students to take part in. Arielle explained about the beach-clean campaign she had been involved with in Cornwall and started to relax.

'Miss Tremain…' A journalist stood up and said that he was from *Fjernland Today*, the principality's most popular newspaper. 'What do you say about the allegations that you were aware that your father Gerran Rowse ran the biggest drug-smuggling operation in Cornwall? At his trial it was proved that millions of pounds' worth of class A drugs were brought in on fishing boats and stashed at the remote cottage where you lived with your father. Yet you stated that you knew nothing of your father's illegal activities.'

'I didn't know…' Arielle tried to defend herself, but no one heard. Her voice had disappeared. She felt faint and gripped the lectern to keep herself standing upright. She could not bring herself to look at Eirik and see the disgust that he must feel for her.

'Furthermore,' the journalist continued, 'a young police constable called Josh Bray was shot and killed by Gerran Rowse, but you told the court that you had not heard the shot that was later proved to have been fired by your father. According to the constable's cousin, Danny Bray, you might not have pulled the trigger, but you were in the cottage when Josh died and as far as his family are concerned you are no better than your scumbag father.'

The room erupted in uproar. The other members of the press who had been invited to the National Council's assembly rushed towards the dais where Arielle was standing and thrust microphones at her. Camera flashbulbs popped. Dimly she heard Eirik yell to the guards. 'Clear the room, *now*.'

## CHAPTER ELEVEN

EIRIK GRABBED ARIELLE and half carried her off the dais. He blinked in the glare of the cameras flashing all around them and knew that pictures of him holding his arm up to protect her from the rabble of journalists and photographers would add fuel to the firestorm that had just taken place. But he did not care. Nothing was more important than getting Arielle out of the assembly room.

'Why the hell didn't you tell me?' he gritted as he pushed her into an empty office and slammed the door shut. She was so pale that he thought she might faint. 'Sit down.' He guided her over to a chair. Her stricken expression evoked a pain beneath his breastbone. She looked *destroyed.*

He wanted to put his arms around her, hold her, but she looked as though she might shatter. He wanted to protect her from the journalist who had made vile accusations against her, from the rest of the goddamned press and their intrusive cameras, from anyone and anything that tried to hurt Arielle. She did not deserve any of it. There was no doubt in his mind. His little mermaid was the sweetest, bravest, most honest woman he had ever known.

*His* Arielle? When had he started to feel possessive as well as protective of her? He shoved a hand through his hair. 'You had better tell me everything,' he said grimly. 'I can't believe you kept secrets from me.'

It felt like a knife in his chest to discover that Arielle had shut him out after he had opened up to her in a way that he'd never done with anyone else except his brother. Niels had been his best friend and confidant, and Eirik realised with a jolt of shock that Arielle was both of those and more to him. He pulled a chair round in front of her and sat down. 'I need answers.'

She swallowed. 'The journalist must have spoken to Danny Bray. There are several strands of the Bray family who have lived in Penash for generations. Josh was Danny's cousin.' Arielle would not look at Eirik. She twisted her fingers together. 'It's true that my father was a major drug dealer, and he… he killed Josh. But I swear I didn't know about the murder or what my father did.'

'I believe you.'

Her green eyes flew to his face. 'You do?' She let out a shaky breath when he nodded. 'People in the village, mainly members of the Bray family, were convinced that I was involved in my father's drug smuggling. I suspected that whatever he did was illegal, and I was sure the smallholding he ran was a cover to hide what he was up to. Strangers used to come to the cottage at night. Every few months my father would disappear for a while. He didn't tell me where he went, but at his trial it emerged that he used the money he made from drug dealing to fund a lavish lifestyle in Dubai. He'd invested in a nightclub there and owned a fleet of flashy cars. At home he always kept one of the outbuildings locked, but once I managed to break in and found a bag containing bank notes. There must have been thousands of pounds. When I asked him about the money he…'

'He what?' Eirik prompted her.

She touched the scar on her cheek. 'He hit me. The blow was so hard that I fell against the edge of the stone fireplace and must have cut my face on a piece of flint.'

Eirik bit back a savage curse. He was filled with murderous rage as he imagined Arielle lying on the floor after her father's blow had sent her flying. 'How old were you?' he asked tautly.

'Fifteen.' She brushed her hand across her eyes. 'He didn't care that he'd hurt me. There was blood everywhere, but he just stood over me and told me that if I ever interfered again, I would get worse than the back of his hand.'

'Where is your father now?' Eirik clenched his fist, wishing he could use it on Arielle's father.

'In prison. He was given a life sentence for murder. Josh Bray was the local police constable. He'd gone to the cottage to question my father about a minor driving offence. But Gerran…' she bit her lip '…I can't bear to call him Dad, had been expecting trouble from another drug dealer, and he shot Josh with his hunting rifle. It came out in the trial that he'd thrown the body over the cliffs, hoping, I guess, that it would be swept out to sea on the tide. But Josh was found, and the bullet mark was linked to my father's gun.'

Arielle stood up and hugged her arms around herself. 'At my father's trial I was questioned about what I knew. I admitted that I had heard a gun fired that night. I didn't go and investigate because I was scared of Gerran. Danny Bray is right,' she choked out. 'If I'd gone downstairs, perhaps I could have helped Josh. But I was too much of a coward to stand up to my father.'

Eirik looked furious, and she could hardly blame him, Arielle thought miserably. The fiasco that had taken place at the National Council's assembly was her fault. She shuddered as a new wave of humiliation swept over her. She was certain that Princess Hulda had arranged for her to be denounced in public and in front of Eirik. Arielle wanted to crawl under a stone.

Eirik had said he believed she had known nothing of her father's crimes, but it did not change the fact that she was the daughter of a murderer. If the media guessed that the future Sovereign of Fjernland was involved with her, especially now when Eirik had just announced that he was not going to marry aristocratic Ida Lundberg, it would not paint him in a good light.

'You shouldn't have been seen with me,' she muttered. 'There are bound to be pictures of us leaving the assembly room together, and people might wonder if there is something going on between us.'

'Don't worry, I'll deal with the press and deny any rumours about us.'

Of course he would. She had been his dirty secret and Eirik would make sure he was not tainted by his association with her. An association that must end immediately. He had been on his phone for the past five minutes, trying to limit the damage to his reputation, no doubt. She did not blame him. Eirik did not want his succession to the throne to be marred by scandal. Although she had not committed any crimes herself, Arielle knew she could never escape the shame of what her father had done.

Eirik finished his call and came over to her. 'How did the journalist know to contact Danny Bray and ask about your past?'

'I suppose Princess Hulda tipped the journalist off,' Arielle mumbled half beneath her breath.

'My mother? Explain what you mean,' he ordered.

'I'd rather not. I don't want to cause trouble between you and your mother.'

Eirik swore. 'Tell me.'

She sighed. 'The Princess knew about our affair and disapproved of me, especially when she found out about my father. She…advised me to break off my relationship with you and leave Fjernland and threatened to tell you about my father if I didn't. She has your best interests at heart,' Arielle said hurriedly when Eirik's expression turned thunderous. 'It is your duty to marry a woman who is suitable to be your Princess Consort. I was only ever a distraction.'

He stared at her as if he was seeing her for the first time. Seeing her for what she was, Arielle thought bleakly. A nobody. There was a knock on the door, and Eirik's private secretary entered the room.

'Sir, I have made all the arrangements you asked for, and you are expected at Sejrrig Place for a meeting with His Serene Highness, Prince Otto. The helicopter is ready for you.'

'Gustav will drive you to the Winter Palace,' Eirik told her. 'I want you to stay there until I am free to come to you, and then we will talk about where we go from here. There are things I need to do first,' he said grimly.

He stepped closer to Arielle, and his eyes blazed into hers. 'Promise you will wait for me.'

She wanted to touch his face, kiss him one last time. Unable to lie to him, she gave a slight dip of her head. Eirik seemed to want to say something else, but then he exhaled heavily and strode out of the room.

Gustav escorted her out of the building via a back door to avoid the press. 'I need to collect some things from my flat,' Arielle told him when he held the car door open for her.

At the marine research institute, she left her resignation letter on Valdemar's desk. She had packed before going to the National Council's assembly and when she emerged from the apartment block carrying her suitcase, Gustav frowned.

'You love Eirik, don't you?' Arielle asked him.

Gustav looked startled for a moment before he nodded. 'I have served the Prince since he was a youth.'

'I love him,' she said softly. 'That's why I need you to take me to the airport. Eirik will be better off without me.'

'I am not sure the Prince will agree.'

'But you know I am right. Eirik must fulfil his destiny for his sake as well as for the people of Fjernland.'

The story had made the international news sites and was the headline on most of Fjernland's newspapers. Leaning back in his seat in the helicopter that was taking him to the Winter Place, Eirik grimaced when he flicked through some advanced copies of the next day's publications. Most had reprinted accounts of Gerran Rowse's trial three years ago. The details of the murder of a young police constable were harrowing. Rowse was a vile individual. In an interview with a neighbour who lived in the Cornish village of Penash, Arielle's father was described as a cruel and violent man.

Eirik thought of the scar on Arielle's face and rage swept through him. Nothing would ever hurt her again. It was his personal mission to make sure of it. She'd be upset if she saw the newspapers, but he would insist that no copies were brought into the Winter Palace. Better still he would take her to his cabin in the mountains, and he planned to keep her distracted in his bed until the story about her father had died down.

Anticipation tugged in his loins. When he made love to her it felt as if they were the only two people in the universe. He had stopped wondering when his desire for her would fade and accepted that he would always want her. And she wanted him too. His nostrils flared as he recalled in erotic detail how she had made love to him with sensual abandon the previous night at the penthouse.

Eirik frowned when he remembered that Arielle had said she was just a distraction for him. Maybe at first it had been true, he acknowledged. He had been under pressure to find a wife and Arielle had been a breath of fresh air compared to the refined young women with pedigrees a mile long his mother had thrown at him.

His eyes narrowed as he thought of his recent, tense conversation with Princess Hulda. He had made it clear to his mother that he would not tolerate her interference in his life, and that if and when he married it would not be because of duty. There was only one reason why two people should marry. Eirik understood that now. But for so long he had convinced himself that he did not need or want emotional attachments.

Following the death of his brother—the only person he had loved with all his heart—a loveless marriage had seemed appealing. He'd decided that he did not want to risk the pain of loving someone again. But a life without risk was dull and grey. He pictured Arielle's vibrant red curls and her sea green eyes. Her smile, and her gentle voice that was a song inside his head. She brought colour and light into his life. The question in his mind was, what was he going to do about her?

The helicopter circled above the Winter Palace and landed on the helipad. When Eirik walked up the steps of the palace a footman opened the door and Maks bounded out to greet him.

Gustav was waiting for him in the entrance hall. 'The dog is delighted to see you, sir,' he commented.

'I'm glad to see him.' Eirik patted his faithful companion's head.

'I fear you will be less glad to see me when I tell you that Miss Tremain…' Gustav hesitated, and premonition dropped into Eirik's stomach like a lead weight.

'What are you going to tell me about her? Where is Arielle?'

'Gone, sir. She said it was for the best.' There was sympathy in the older man's eyes. 'I'm sorry.'

Arielle pushed open the door of the pub. It was busy inside. The trawlermen had returned after several days at sea, and some of them looked as though they had been drinking all afternoon. No one took any notice of her as she walked up to the bar, carrying a few of her mother's paintings.

When she had bumped into the landlady of the Sailor's Rest in the local supermarket a few days ago,

Arielle had mentioned that she was moving away from Penash.

'I don't blame you, love,' Julie had told her. 'It's no place for a young woman, living in that remote cottage. I hear that the owners who leased it to your father are planning to turn it into a bed and breakfast. I wouldn't mind a couple of your mum's paintings. She was a good artist and painted some lovely seascapes.'

There was a crowd of drinkers standing in front of the bar and Arielle tried to squeeze past them. 'Well, look what the cat's dragged in,' said a familiar voice.

'Shut up, Tamara,' Danny Bray muttered to his sister. Arielle did not understand why he was defending her. It was because of what Danny had told the journalist that she had fled from Fjernland.

'Well, I think you've got a nerve coming in here,' Tamara told Arielle. 'After what your father did.'

'Yes, what my father did, not me.' Anger rushed like scalding lava through Arielle. She'd had enough of being voiceless and picked on by the Brays and others who blamed her for crimes she hadn't committed. The pub grew quiet, and everyone stared at her. Good. Let them stare.

She pushed her windswept curls off her face and looked around the pub. 'Most of you have known me since I was a baby. I went to school with some of you, and all of you—*all of you*—knew what my father was like. He was a violent bully and he treated me badly. But not one person in Penash tried to help me or questioned whether Gerran Rowse should be allowed to bring up a child after my mum died. You accused me of being involved in my father's crimes, but I had no part in his disgusting drug dealing. As for poor Josh Bray…' her voice trembled '…I wish I could have saved him, but I was terrified of my father. I will regret for ever that I was a coward.'

'Never a coward, *skatta*. You are the most courageous person I have ever known, and a million times braver than everyone in this room.'

Arielle heard Eirik's voice but told herself she must have imagined it. He wasn't here in Penash. He couldn't be.

The crowd of drinkers in the pub moved aside and she stared at the impossibly handsome man who was standing in the doorway. His dark blond hair was ruffled as though he'd been running his fingers through it, although now he had shoved his hands into the pockets of his jeans, which had the effect of drawing her attention to his hard thighs.

'He's a prince,' someone said. 'Of that principality called Ferneyland or something.'

A few people bowed, and the pub landlady, Julie, came round the bar and curtseyed. 'We've never had a royal visitor in the Sailor's Rest before. I'd be honoured to get you a drink, Your Highness.'

'Thank you, but there is only one reason I am here.' Eirik's blue eyes blazed across the distance of the pub and held Arielle's startled gaze. 'I would like to talk to you, Arielle,' he said intently. 'Will you come with me, *elskeda*?'

She couldn't move, and her heart was thumping so

hard that she was surprised it wasn't visible through her tee shirt.

'Go on, lass.' Julie nudged her, taking the paintings that Arielle was still holding out of her trembling fingers. Convinced that this was all a dream, she walked towards Eirik and followed him outside.

'You shouldn't be here.' She forced her voice to work.

'I had to come. You didn't go to the Winter Place and wait for me as I'd asked you to,' he reminded her, sounding oddly tense.

She lifted her chin. 'The last time I was there for the masquerade ball you had me smuggled into the palace secretly. I won't be hidden away or feel that I am a dirty secret ever again.'

'I'm sorry I made you feel like that. I want you to come back to Fjernland and I swear that you will only ever be treated with the respect you deserve.'

Her heart ached. 'I don't belong in your world.'

'You *are* my world.' Eirik held out his hand to her. 'Will you listen to what I have to say? If you decide that there is no future for us, I will respect your choice, even though it will kill me,' he said tautly.

He was talking in riddles. But she would agree to travel to the ends of the earth to spend five more minutes with him. When she put her hand in his, he gripped her fingers tightly. They walked down the cobbled street towards the harbour in silence. Arielle let him lead her aboard a small motorboat and her sense of unreality grew when he cast off and the boat chugged out of the harbour.

The sky was cornflower blue, and the May sunshine was warm on her face as the boat skimmed across the bay. The breeze ruffled the blond hairs on Eirik's forearms as he steered the boat. Arielle took the opportunity while he was looking straight ahead to drink in his chiselled features. He turned his head towards her, and his smile stole her breath. How she loved him! She quickly broke eye contact, afraid that he would see her emotions that she must hide from him.

She recognised this part of the coastline and minutes later they arrived at Pixie Cove. Eirik dropped the anchor and jumped over the side of the boat into the shallow water. Arielle made to follow him, but he scooped her into his arms and carried her up the beach. It felt so good to be held by him once again and feel his heart thudding erratically beneath her ear when she rested her head against his chest. As he lowered her to her feet, her body brushed against his and he groaned and hauled her closer.

'I told myself I would be patient and court you,' he rasped. 'But when you are in my arms, I can't think of anything but how much I want to do this…'

Eirik brought his mouth down on hers and with a helpless sigh Arielle responded to his kiss, parting her lips to allow his tongue to probe between them. She had left Fjernland a week ago, but it felt like a lifetime without him and for a few moments she was lost in the beauty and passion of his kiss.

But reality returned and she eased away from him. They were both breathing hard. 'You shouldn't have done that,' she choked out. 'Why have you brought me here?'

'This is where it began,' he said softly. 'I was saved from the sea by a mermaid. But in return for my life, she stole my heart.'

'Eirik...don't say such things.' Tears filled her eyes. 'We can never be together.'

'We will never be apart again.' He slid his hand beneath her chin and tilted her face up to his. 'Don't cry, *min elskeda*.'

A tear rolled down her cheek. 'You were angry when I told you about my father.'

'My anger was not with you.' His face twisted as if he were in pain. '*Faen*, when you told me that your father had hit you and was responsible for this—' he brushed his thumb gently over the scar on her cheek '—I felt so much rage and hatred for him. I wished I had been there to protect you as you should have been protected by the local community.'

'Gerran can't hurt anyone now.' But her father's notoriety would always cast a shadow on her life, Arielle thought bleakly. She bit her lip. 'Why did Danny Bray defend me in the pub?'

'I threatened to sue him for libel if he breathed a word against you ever again. When Bray realised that he faced being fined hundreds of thousands of pounds it made him reconsider his behaviour. |I have also taken out an injunction banning the media from printing anything defamatory about you.'

'But everything Danny said about my father is

true and you can't stop the story from being in the newspapers.'

He smiled. 'It is old news already since a volcano named Vredkaempen erupted two days ago. Angry Giant, to give it its English name, is miles away from any towns, and no one was affected,' he assured her. 'The newspapers in Fjernland are full of reports about the volcano.'

Eirik slipped his hand into his pocket and withdrew a silk pouch. He tipped the contents out and held up a silver chain, which was attached to a pink pendant, carved into the shape of a heart. Arielle's breath caught when she recognised it was the piece of sea glass that she'd found smashed in her studio. She'd guessed that Danny Bray and some of his cronies had been responsible for the damage.

'You had told me that you found the sea glass when you were with your mother, and it reminded you of her,' Eirik explained. 'I asked a jeweller to create the pendant so that you can wear it close to your heart.'

'It's beautiful.' She studied the pink glass heart mistily, trying and failing to hold back her tears. 'Why did you do such a lovely thing for me?'

'Because I love you,' he said huskily.

Arielle's heart stopped beating. She lifted her gaze to Eirik's face and the tender expression in his eyes made her tremble. 'You said you had no intention of falling in love,' she whispered.

He gave her a strained smile as he lifted his hand and brushed a stray curl off her face. 'And yet here I am, completely and utterly in love with you, *elskeda*. I think I have been since the last time we were here at Pixie Cove, and I know I will love you for ever.'

Arielle's mind was whirling. Happiness hovered within her grasp, but she dared not reach out for it. 'You can't,' she choked out.

Eirik wiped the tears from her cheeks with his thumb pads. 'Don't you want me to love you?' There was uncertainty in his voice, the vulnerability of the boy he'd once been who had yearned for his parents' affection.

'Of course I do, more than anything in the world.' She put her hand on his jaw and trembled again when he turned his face and kissed her palm. 'I love you with all my heart. But loving you is agony. I want to be able to love you freely and publicly.' Her voice cracked. 'Please don't ask me to be your secret mistress after you marry the woman who will be your Princess Consort.'

Eirik caught her to him and held her against his big chest. 'I don't want you to be my mistress, *min elskeda*. I want you to be my wife.'

She stared at him in disbelief and dawning wonder that he did truly love her. But love was not enough. He was bound by duty and centuries-old tradition. 'Oh, my darling, we both know that can never happen. I can't marry you. The people of Fjernland will never accept me, and your mother certainly won't.' Arielle pressed her finger against his lips when he made to speak. 'I cannot change who my father is and the terrible crimes he committed. You must choose a bride who is suitable to be a princess.'

Eirik's eyes blazed. '*You* are my Princess, and only you. The Fjernlandic people will fall in love with you as I did. As for my mother…' His jaw hardened. 'Princess Hulda is praying that you will accept my proposal because I have made it clear to her and Prince Otto that no other woman will be my wife.'

He took the sea-glass pendant and secured the chain around Arielle's neck. 'I will only marry for love, and I will only ever love you,' he said softly. 'I have persuaded my father and the National Council to change the principality's constitution so that if I die without an heir, Fjernland won't be returned to Danish rule. Instead, the democratically elected National Council will choose a head of state to lead the government.'

'Can you do that?'

'It's done, and it was surprisingly easy. But you can understand why my mother is desperate for you to agree to marry me, and for us to have children.' Eirik smiled at her stunned expression. 'I would like to have a family with you, not because I want an heir, but because I adore you and I'd love to have three or four mini versions of you.'

'Four!' Arielle stopped trying to fight the joy that swept through her, stopped being afraid to grab hold of the happiness that was standing right there in front of her in the form of a golden prince. Her Prince. Her fairy-tale happy ending.

'We don't have to have four, or any children at all if you don't want them,' Eirik said hastily.

'I do want your babies,' she assured him before she pulled his face down to hers and kissed him, telling him without words everything that was in her heart. 'But more than anything I want you to love me as much as I love you, for the rest of our lives.'

He captured her hand and pressed it to his chest above his heart. 'It beats only for you. Always and for ever, *elskeda*. My love,' he translated for her.

'Eirik…?' Arielle was sure she was dreaming when he dropped down onto one knee on the sand and took a small velvet box from his pocket. He opened it to reveal an exquisite, square-cut pink sapphire surrounded by diamonds that sparkled in the sunshine.

'Arielle, will you marry me and be my wife, my companion, my princess and my dearest love in this life and beyond?'

'I will,' she whispered. And then more loudly, because she had found her voice and would never lose it again. 'I will love you to eternity.'

Eirik slid the engagement ring onto her finger and stood up to draw her into his arms. He kissed her tenderly and with increasing passion until they were both shaking. 'Did you say that Pixie Cove is completely secluded?' he murmured.

'Yes, very few people know it's here.'

'Good.' He tugged her tee shirt over her head and

unclipped her bra, giving a low groan as her breasts spilled into his hands. 'Because I have plans for us for the rest of the day and I don't want to be disturbed, my love.'

# EPILOGUE

EIRIK STROLLED ACROSS the white sand on the private beach. Behind him stood an impressive castle that was the royal residence of Princess Catalina of San Sabinus and the Princess's new husband, an Italian Count, Bruno Oliveto. The principality was close to the heel of Italy, set in the azure-blue Adriatic Sea. The beach had a natural tidal pool surrounded by rocks that made it a safe place for children to swim.

Currently there were three mermaids in the pool. The two younger ones splashed in the water with their silver monofin tails as they swam. They were identical twins, with strawberry-blonde hair and deep blue eyes that appeared to be green in certain lights. The third mermaid was sitting on a rock. Her long hair was drying into titian curls and her sparkly green tail matched her bikini top. Eirik felt a familiar tug of desire as he studied his wife's voluptuous curves. Arielle's breasts were fuller now that she was halfway through her second pregnancy. A boy this time, but their son would not be Eirik's heir. In the future, Fjernland would be ruled jointly by his daughters, Princess Anna, and Princess Josefine.

'Papa, will you come and swim with us?'

'Look how fast I can swim. I'm faster than Anna.'

'No, you're not.'

'Girls,' their mother said softly. 'No arguing on the last day of our holiday.'

Eirik watched his little mermaids dive down to the bottom of the pool. 'Three years old and they are already amazing swimmers.' He waded through the pool to Arielle, the love of his life and the epicentre of his world. 'Will you mind going back to Fjernland tomorrow?' Royal duties took up much of their time, but they made sure that family time came first.

'Of course not.' Arielle lifted her face for his kiss. 'I don't mind where I am as long as I am with you.' It was a sentiment Eirik shared. 'The wedding was lovely, wasn't it?' She smiled. 'Catalina looked so happy with Bruno.'

'It reminded me of our wedding.' There had been three days of national holiday in Fjernland in celebration of the royal wedding, which had taken place in the Winter Palace. Eirik would never forget how his heart had leapt in his chest when he'd seen his bride walking towards him, an ethereal vision in an exquisite ivory lace wedding gown. Arielle was his princess in every way, and a month after they were married she had worn a fabulous diamond and sapphire tiara and stood by his side as the Princess Consort when he had been enthroned as Fjernland's

Reigning Sovereign following Prince Otto's abdication.

His thoughts returned to the present as Arielle laid her hand on his jaw. 'Lina told me that she will always keep the memory of your brother in a little corner of her heart.'

'Niels would have wanted her to be happy,' Eirik said with certainty.

'Are you happy?' Arielle asked gently.

He smiled at his beloved. 'Do you need to ask? You are my life, you and the girls, and our son when he is born.' Family. They meant the world to him. Time had helped to heal the pain of his brother's death. He too would always carry Niels's memory in his heart.

Eirik stood up and looked across the tidal pool and beyond to the ocean. A flash of silver caught his eye and he thought he glimpsed a tail. It had been too big to belong to a fish. Of course, mermaids and mermen couldn't really exist. Could they?

* * * * *

*If* Her Secret Royal Dilemma *swept you off your feet, then don't miss these other Chantelle Shaw stories!*

Her Wedding Night Negotiation
Housekeeper in the Headlines
The Greek Wedding She Never Had
Nine Months to Tame the Tycoon
The Italian's Bargain for His Bride

*Available now!*

COMING NEXT MONTH FROM

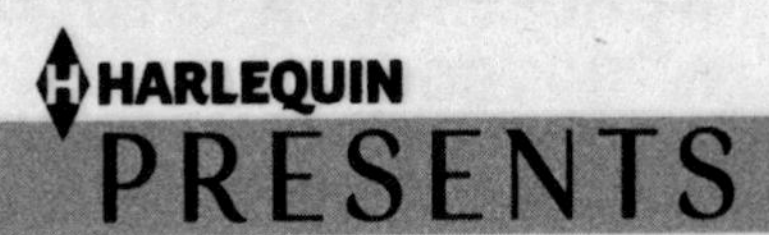


**#4025 THE BILLIONAIRE'S BABY NEGOTIATION**

by Millie Adams

Innocent Olive Monroe has hated Icelandic billionaire Gunnar Magnusson for years...and then she discovers the consequences of their electric night together. Now she's facing the highest-stakes negotiation of all—Gunnar wants their baby, her company and Olive!

**#4026 MAID FOR THE GREEK'S RING**

by Louise Fuller

Achileas Kane sees himself as living proof that wedding vows are meaningless. But this illegitimate son can only gain his inheritance if he weds. His proposal to hotel chambermaid Effie Price is simply a contract—until they seal their contract with a single sizzling kiss...

**#4027 THE NIGHT THE KING CLAIMED HER**

by Natalie Anderson

King Felipe knows far too much about the scandalous secrets in Elsie Wynter's past. But with her stranded in his palace for one night only, and their mutual desire flaring, he can think of nothing but finally claiming her...

**#4028 BOUND BY A NINE-MONTH CONFESSION**

by Cathy Williams

Celia is unprepared for the passion she finds with billionaire Leandro, let alone finding herself holding a positive pregnancy test weeks later! Now they have nine months to decide if their connection can make them a family.

## #4029 CROWNING HIS KIDNAPPED PRINCESS

*Scandalous Royal Weddings*

by Michelle Smart

When daring Prince Marcelo Berruti rescues Clara Sinclair from a forced wedding, he makes international headlines. Now he's facing a diplomatic crisis...unless he claims the beautiful bride-to-be himself!

## #4030 DESTITUTE UNTIL THE ITALIAN'S DIAMOND

by Julia James

Lana can't believe the crushing debts her ex left her with are forcing her to make a convenient marriage with ruthless Italian Salvatore. But while her head agrees to take his name, her body craves his forbidden touch!

## #4031 INNOCENT IN HER ENEMY'S BED

by Dani Collins

Ilona is aware that Leander will do anything for revenge against her stepfamily. She just never pictured herself becoming his ally. Or that the sensual back-and-forth between them would lead to their marriage bed...

## #4032 HIS DESERT BRIDE BY DEMAND

by Lela May Wight

Desert prince Akeem wants to show first love Charlotte what she gave up by turning her back on him. Then their secret tryst threatens to become a scandal, and duty-bound Akeem must make an outrageous demand: she'll be his queen!

---

*Desert prince Akeem wants to show first love Charlotte what she gave up by turning her back on him. Then their secret tryst threatens to become a scandal, and duty-bound Akeem must make an outrageous demand: she'll be his queen!*

*Read on for a sneak preview of Lela May Wight's next story for Harlequin Presents*
His Desert Bride by Demand

"Can you explain what happened?" Akeem asked. "The intensity?"

Could she? Nine years had passed between them—a lifetime—and still… No, she couldn't.

"My father had a lifetime of being reckless for his own amusement—"

"And you wanted a taste of it?"

"No," he denied, his voice a harsh rasp.

"Then what did you want?" Charlotte pushed.

"A night—"

"You risked your reputation for a night?" She cut him off, her insides twisting. "And so far, it's been a disaster, and we haven't even got to bed." She blew out a puff of agitated air.

"Make no mistake," he warned, "things have changed."

"Changed?"

"My bed is off-limits."

She laughed, a throaty gurgle. "How dare you pull me from my life, fly me who knows how many miles into a kingdom I've never heard of and turn my words back on me!" She fixed him with an exasperated glare. "How dare you try to turn the tables on me!"

"If the tables have turned on anyone," he corrected, "it is me because you will be my wife."





HPEXP0622